Nick Storie Mysteries
Book 3b
The Wedding

Nick marries Janet and receives a wedding present from DeGulio, who is charged with murder when Nick returns from his honeymoon

Critic comment;
Quite good. Above average. Interesting selection of characters. While it's no literary masterpiece, it's not hack, either. Well worth buying. – GGL

Nick Storie Mysteries
Book 3b
The Wedding
© 1989 & 2019 by C. D. Moulton

This is a work of fiction. Any resemblances to persons, living or dead, or events is purely coincidental unless otherwise stated.

The Wedding

About the author

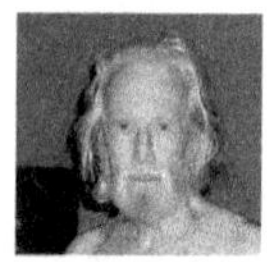

CD was born in Lakeland, Florida, in 1938. He is educated in genetics and botany. He has traveled over much of the world, particularly when he was in music as a rock rhythm guitarist with some well-known bands in the late sixties and early seventies. He has worked as a high steel worker and as a longshoreman, clerk, orchidist, bar owner, salvage yard manager and landscaper – among other things.

CD began writing fiction in 1984 and has more than 300 books published as of 3/15/16 in SciFi, murder, orchid culture and various other fields.

He now resides in Puerto Armuelles, David, and Gualaca, Chiriqui, Panamá, where he continues research into epiphytic plants and plays music with friends. He loves the culture of the indigenous people and counts a majority of his closer friends among that group. Several have "adopted" him as their father. He funds those he can afford through the universities where they have all excelled. "The Indios are very intelligent people, they are simply too poor (in material things and money. Culturally, they are very wealthy) to pursue higher education."

CD loves Panamá and the people, despite horrendous experiences (Free e-book; *Fading Paradise*). He plans to spend the rest of his life in the paradise that is Panamá

- Estrelita Suarez V. de Jaramillo – 3/15/2016

CD is involved in research of natural cancer cure at this time. It has proven effective in all cases, so far. It is based on a plant that has been in use for thousands of years, is safe, available, and cheap. He has studied botany, and was cured of a serious lymphoma with use of the plant, *Ambrosia peruviana*.

Information about this cure is free on the FaceBook group, Natural medicine research. CD asks only that all who try it please report on its effectiveness on that group.

The Wedding

Nick and Janet Storie ran laughing through the hail of rice. Nick's buddy and brother homicide cop, Lt. Jim Hill, stood at the end of the line with his own wife. Capt. "Paddy" James and his wife stood across from them. Ed Goins, also a cop, was at one side of the first of the line next to Janet's parents. Across from them were Marsha and Hank Blevins.

Sgt. Marsha was aide and private secretary to Paddy. Everyone acknowledged she was the real power in the division.

Shirley Kiser, desk sgt. at South Station, stood with Dr.s "Tiny" Menthorne and David Klein, the coroners. Lonnie Micks was at the car with a beautiful girl, all strawberry curls, and the guys from "Not So Hard Times," the famous rock band and their wives and girlfriends stood to the side. Two of them played acoustic guitars and serenaded the scene with a song Ben Hard, ex-lead singer, wrote for the occasion.

They would all meet in Sarasota at Janet's parents' home for the reception, then Janet and Nick would sneak away to their honeymoon. They had purposely not given anyone a hint as to where they might be going for the week.

There were a lot of people at the reception, and the gifts were amazing. They were given earlier, but Janet's parents had put them on a big table at the reception because they knew some of the party had waited until then to bring the gifts and they didn't want to embarrass anyone who didn't know the proper time to present wedding gifts. This meant they could simply add their gifts to the table and no one the wiser.

Nick had worked with some very wealthy people at

times in his role as night shift homicide cop. He almost always ended up being friends with even those he caught.

There was one manila envelope on the corner of the table that had not been there a few minutes before Nick and Janet started to unwrap the presents. Janet's mother was making careful notes as to what was given and by whom, because Janet would want to send thank you notes to everyone as soon as they got back from the honeymoon.

Nick picked it up, noted it was addressed to "The Stories," and tore it open.

It seemed to be a deed of some sort, written in French.

Janet was fluent in a number of languages, so she read it over and announced they were apparently the new owners of a small oceanfront property and all facilities thereon permanently affixed – on the island of Martinique!

"We can't accept anything like that!" Nick declared. "Who sent it?"

He shook the envelope and a little slip dropped out. He picked it up to read:

Dearest Nickie,

Please do not think of refusing this. It is a place in my heart where I possibly may never go again. Our somewhat differing philosophies have points in each of our favor. This one is to yours.

The cost is nothing to me, as you well know. I would never insult a friend with money. This is the kind of place I deeply love, and am certain you will, too. You will be pleasantly surprised at how well I know you when you see the place.

I want you to have this. Enjoy it and think maybe El Jefe isn't all bad. I am sorry our differences disallow my

Lonnie was standing next to Nick. He said, "Wasn't he that drug lord?"

"Uh-huh! We invited him, didn't we?"

"Yes," Janet replied. "You wanted me to meet him."

"What will you do?" Lonnie asked.

"Jan? How would you like to change honeymoon plans a bit? Go maybe a little farther south?" Nick asked, swinging her around.

"You will *not* accept any such present from such as DeGulio!" Paddy demanded. "I would, but you will *not*!"

"So would I!" Janet replied, laughing. "It's to both of us, so I'm accepting!"

"Nick, don't you ever become obligated to DeGulio's type!" Paddy begged.

"No, Paddy, there *is* no obligation! Believe me, Pancho wouldn't do this if he dreamed I'd even suspect there was any such thing behind it.

"I really wish you could meet him."

"Nick, if there's ever any hint of a connection, I'm obligated to noting it," Paddy warned seriously. "I know you wouldn't ... you have to be careful of appearances."

"I'll give it back to him after we stay there. I could never hope to pay the taxes on that kind of place on a cop's salary. Pancho will understand that."

"I hope you know what you're doing!" Paddy sighed.

"You don't have to worry about Nick!" Lonnie said.

"One thing I'll insist on," Marsha put in.

"What's that, Marsh?" Nick asked.

"That you don't give that place back 'til *after* my vacation! I want to go to one romantic paradise island one time in my life with the one perfect dream man!

"I can do all that except the last thing, so I'll take Hank!"

"Deal!" Nick grinned.

He and Janet finished the gifts and mingled for a bit, then Nick sneaked back into the den to call Pancho.

"Nickie! You should be away by now, not calling your friends!" Pancho greeted. "I am so pleased you thought enough of me to call."

"Pancho, I can't accept that gift. I'm going to spend the honeymoon there, but it's way too much. Really!"

"Nickie, it isn't. I promise you. I know you very well, because we are very much alike. I think I know your bride very well because I know you, though I've never met her.

"Wait 'til you see the place! It's a complete paradise to me and will be to you!

"Nick, trust me? You have my word."

"Janet wants the place. I wish you were here. I want my friends to meet you.

"You were invited, Pancho. You could have come."

"Nickie, if I had come other people would soon have come. They are people neither of us wish to associate with in any way. They would not be there, but they also would.

"That is why I can't again go to my private little piece of paradise. My presence there would change it from a paradise to a much worse place, not because of me, rather because of who and what would inevitably follow. I will not do that to a place – or person – I love.

"I ached in my heart when I received the invitation, but I could find no way.

"I am there in spirit, Nickie. Your call puts me there

even more, in its own way.

"When you see your hideaway, you'll understand how well I know you!

"Now! Get back to your bride!"

"Thank you, Pancho. I wish you were here. It's not possible for us to be friends at all, much less for me to consider you such a good friend. Perhaps one of my closest.

"Thank you for caring."

They said goodbye and Nick went back into the reception. About two hours later he and Janet sneaked out with the help of Lonnie and Jim.

What an incongruous situation! He'd spoken to Don Francisco "Pancho" DeGulio, better known as "El Jefe," exactly twice in person! There had been an automatic respect and understanding between them. Immediately.

DeGulio was a drug lord and Nick was a cop, yet the respect they knew for one another was immense. Nick had the guts to go to a party at DeGulio's Boca Raton place, saunter in, and ask the bartender to announce he wanted a word. He'd gone so far as to tell the bartender he was a cop.

No one had ever done anything vaguely like that before. Pancho was amused, then greatly respected Nick for that. There was a deep seriousness in the meeting, but it was humorous on another level. Both of them saw the humor in the situation. Both of them enjoyed that humor and knew trust of one another because of it. The humor caused some kind of bonding and acceptance.

Now they were friends. It was a friendship neither had wanted nor sought, but it was there and it was very real. It was strong enough that neither ever considered there would ever be the least possibility of compromising his separate personal code. Nick was a homicide cop and

Pancho was a drug lord. Pancho would be very careful to prevent pressure on the friendship because of that. His business would never involve Nick. Period.

Pancho's philosophy told him what he was doing was the only thing he *could* do. His people and his family in another country were impoverished and held impotent because of centuries of oppressive politicians and dictators. The drugs gave them an economic base, thus a power base from which to improve their lot. The fact that another country had so many problems related to the product was, to him, THEIR problem. His first responsibility was to his own people.

Francisco DeGulio was an honorable man.

Nick Storie was equally an honorable man.

Nick'ss foremost responsibility was to his people. He could see a conflict DeGulio could not. He understood Pancho's very real arguments. He even agreed with a hell of a lot more of them than he liked to admit. People who used those drugs had ample knowledge of what they could be getting into before they ever used them, which was why Nick never had. He had little sympathy for those who cry and moan about an addiction they brought on their own heads. So far as both men were concerned, those types weren't worth the powder to blow them to hell (which happened far too often), anyhow.

What DeGulio didn't understand, in Nick's point of view, was that those refuse inflicted their criminal violence and thievery on innocent people. *That* is the bad part.

Pancho looked on it as a matter where he supplied the drugs or someone else did. He gave most of the profits – far more than anyone guessed – back to his own people. Others probably wouldn't be bothered by anything past personal greed.

What the two did totally agree on was that if the USA spent half what they spend fighting those drugs in helping people fighting to barely survive under oppressive dictatorships of one kind or another there wouldn't *be* any large drug problem. It seemed to Nick his own government spent far to much effort in shoring up dictators and far too little in helping their victims.

That was the basis of understanding between them. Nick was Nick. Pancho was Pancho. They were both absolutely honorable men. The only difference between them was in the code of that honor.

There really wasn't much. What there was was critical.

Janet squealed in purest delight at her first sight of their private honeymoon palace. Nick grinned to himself and murmured a silent, "So you know me that well! Thanks, Pancho!"

There was about a five acre plot of lush tropical forest that covered a small hill with a little cabin with a thatched roof atop the knoll. The third of the property to the east ended at the ocean and was covered in stately coconut palms with myriad amazingly varied and bright flowering plants beneath. A little stream burbled along the south property line.

"Oh, Nick! I'm so relieved! You told me about that huge mansion Pancho lives in in Boca Raton and I kept picturing one of those villas in Southern France being here.

"Oh, Nick! This is so *perfect*!"

"Pancho is a very simple person. He could see I am, too. I'd hate some big, gaudy thing.

"He told me it was a hideaway!

"The taxes on this place are nonexistent. We can afford

to keep it.

"Can you picture Lonnie here?"

Lonnie Micks was an extraordinarily handsome man. He was a landscape genius, and seemed to fit among plants. He wore almost nothing, most times.

The women called him their Pan. They couldn't stay away from him. He actually enjoyed the attention, but was unself-conscious about his beauty. He seemed unaware of it, usually.

"We'll have to let all our friends use the place. Lonnie can be one of the first ones. In two weeks he'll have the place arranged so it looks like a painting of a dream – well, it does anyhow, but you know what I mean – and everything will look exactly like it grew there naturally.

"Let's go see what our palace is like inside!"

The cabin was three rooms and a bath. There was a small gas run generator to run a pump for the water and to run a few lights and appliances. The refrigerator ran on kerosene, which there was a fiberglass fifty five gallon drum of outside. The stove also burned kerosene, which worried Nick a bit, but it was well-vented and the food didn't get any oily flavor from it. It didn't stink.

The sea was much cleaner than Nick thought water could be. The climate was perfect, making for a slow, lazy pace to life. It rained lightly almost every after-noon, but the rain was warm and friendly. They didn't usually bother to go inside out of it.

Both Nick and Janet liked to fish. There were all kinds of other seafoods in the area. They ate well.

"You know something?" Nick asked as they stood on the hill above their property as they left, "I owe Pancho big time for this!"

"You don't owe him anything!" Janet replied sharply. "Don't start thinking like that, Nick. It'll ruin it. For him!"

"I didn't mean like that. "I mean I'm someday going to have to find the perfect gift for him. The only things I can think of are beyond my reach.

"He cares about his people. I can't do anything about them."

"I don't agree! I think there's something you *can* give him. Nick! This was his hideaway. It was his place to come to be away from the sordidity of life!

"He can't come here again because he's afraid those hoods he's forced to deal with will come, but He can go to someplace where they already are! There is still one paradise place he can go!

"Lonnie won't mind."

Nick looked thoughtful. "If there's any way he can give all those punks the slip it could work!"

Lonnie really wouldn't mind. He and Pancho would get along fabulously well. They were both philosophical people, but Lonnie wasn't nearly so fatalistic as Pancho.

Nick was thoughtful all the way back to the states. He had to find a way to make it work!

Chapter ten

"Paddy? I just called to say we're back, but I don't expect to be called unless there's a real emergency!" Nick greeted on his return Sunday night.

He was calling Paddy at home.

"Nick? Have you heard?" Paddy asked.

"Heard what? Paddy, you sound ... strange!"

"It's Pancho DeGulio. He was arrested for murder late Friday afternoon. Jessup called from DEA, Miami, to gloat about it."

"What's the setup?" Nick hissed through his teeth, after a shocked pause.

"He's not a citizen, so no bail. He's being held in Miami. According to Jessup, he killed some woman named Sylvia Perez in a domestic quarrel."

"No damned way!"

"Jessup says the real reason is that she knew too much about his operation and was trying to blackmail him. Frankly, Nick, Jessup is a good bit too smug and self-serving about this. I don't think he killed her and I think Jessup knows it.

"You know how I feel about the likes of DeGulio. I'm also very strong on law. I have my opinion about cops who stretch the rules.

"DeGulio hasn't mentioned your name in any context whatever. I don't suppose he would.

"You have another week on your honeymoon leave. Will Janet understand?"

"I think so, Paddy. She knows how I am about my friends.

"Will you authorize me to act over there on some pretense?"

"Blaine's in charge over there. I know you well enough to figure what you'll do, so you're assigned to his department temporarily.

"You owe DeGulio favors, and Blaine owes me some.

"Be very careful with this one, Nick."

"You know I will. Paddy, I don't owe Pancho anything. He would hate for anyone to think that."

"I think I actually believe that! Take extreme care. I don't have time to train another officer right now."

"Thanks, Paddy." They hung up.

"What am I going to understand?"

"That DEA jerk, Jessup, set something up. Paddy says he got suspicious right away because of the way he gloated.

"Honey, they've arrested Pancho. For murder."

"Oh, Nick!" she cried. She paused and held to him a minute, then said, "I'll pack some things. You arrange the flight.

"I suppose my going's out of the question?"

"You know the kind of people I'll have to be dealing with."

She nodded, bit her lip, and went to look through his clothes. He called the airlines.

"Paddy twisted my arm just a bit, but I get a bit tight-jawed when some federal agency tells me how to run my department," Blaine explained. "Maybe DEA has the goods on DeGulio, or maybe it's fairytale time. You know the kinds of things they can do.

"All I know about Mr. DeGulio is that he'd drop one word if somebody started giving me any trouble and it would *stop*!

"He'll be in visitors' cell B. You might be careful what you say in there."

"But it isn't legal to listen in those rooms!" Nick snarled sharply, then nodded and continued, "I get it!

That's part of the pressure the feds are giving you?"

Blaine made a tight sour face and replied, "Why, Officer Storie! Whatever made you say a thing like that?"

Nick nodded and was led to a small room. Pancho was seated at a bench and looked up as he came in. His eyes widened. "Nickie! How kind of you to come! I didn't expect you back yet!"

"Neither did Jessup. Be careful of what you say.

"Tell me what happened?"

"You didn't meet Sylvia, did you? She was in the room with my employee and me the first time we met, but I believe she left just before introductions were made.

"She was a very special friend. Perhaps she would someday have become my wife. A man could do far worse.

"I was out on my boat from last Thursday noon until shortly past noon on Friday. When we came in the police were waiting on the dock. Sylvia had been killed. There was a bomb in her car. I was arrested on an anonymous tip. Some person claimed he saw me doing something to her car and my fingerprints were found on the vehicle.

"Considering that I bought the automobile for her and often was a passenger in it, that hardly surprises me."

"You didn't kill her? You didn't hire anyone else to kill her?"

"I think you know that I did not. I give you my word, Nickie. I did nothing to harm her or to cause anyone else to do so. I would not. She was special and dear to me.

"I will ask that you find who did. As a friend."

"I'm here to do exactly that. I don't think they have sufficient evidence to hold you. I'll see that you're treated fairly.

"Paddy told me minutes before I came over here that he can't countenance a crooked cop. I can't either, and I think there's one in the woodwork here!"

"Mr. Jessup simply does his job as he sees it. Perhaps he is a bit zealous, but he's not truly crooked, Nickie."

"Not purposely. – *maybe*. It comes to the same thing. He made an oath to uphold the law, and that means he can't be the one to break that law without doubling his offense – through the perjury he committed when taking that oath!"

"Nickie? Please. Do not allow this thing to become a personal vendetta. He is much like me in some ways. He seeks a way to an end."

"There's a vast difference in one way, Pancho. You never took an oath to stay within the law."

Pancho gave Nick a long deeply speculative look, then smiled.

"Nickie, be very careful. I swear to you here there is nothing to fear from my people, but not only my people are involved in this thing. Comprende?"

"Si. Comprende, mi amigo."

"Why come to me?" Jessup asked. "It's a job for the local cops to handle."

"Because you've put pressure on the local cops," Nick replied. "I'd think there was enough evidence around now about how that usually turns out that you wouldn't try it."

"We got along pretty good before. Why pull this crap now? What's changed? You get a little too friendly with DeGulio, take expensive gifts, and feel you've got to protect him? Gonna start a little personal vendetta against me?

"Like he says, we're a lot alike."

"Let's get one thing straight, you arrogant two-bit son of a bitch! You don't intimidate me! You learned that when I was here before.

"Pancho and I are friends, but that has nothing to do with my job.

"You tried to set me up when I was here before. You sent me out there as some kind of a joke just to see what would happen. You used me the one and only time you ever will!

"If anything I've said in a secure room ever becomes known I'll have *you* before a federal court, and I'll see that every single damned conviction you ever got's overturned! Comprende?

"Don't say you don't have it wired, Pal! You just used word-for-word the same thing Pancho said in that room!

"So! I also said you're a crooked cop. You've proven *that*! In spades!"

"Now hang on, you!" Jessup was red-faced. "No matter what you think, DeGulio's responsible for a hell of a lot of dope on the streets! If he killed that broad or not, we've got him for it!

"He and I think alike! I want him off the streets, this gets him off. Mission accomplished!"

"You leave out one little item there, don't you? Maybe there's a little thing you didn't even consider?

"Send him up for the murder he didn't commit and the one who *did* commit it walks! If the real killer does it again, what did you accomplish, other than becoming an accessory?

"There's one huge difference in the way you think and the way Pancho thinks. I said that in the room that you illegally bugged: He didn't swear any oath about following the law. You did. Had Pancho sworn such an oath he'd literally die before he broke that oath, while you consider your own sworn oath, your word, merely a convenience to be followed or not depending on your mood at the moment.

"In other words Pancho is an honorable man.

"You're as certainly not!"

"You stay out of my way! I'll hang your ass out to dry if you interfere!"

"*One* of us is going to be hung out to dry! It remains to be seen *which* one!"

He slammed out of the office. He hoped he'd accomplished what he wanted there. It was mostly an act, but he had to force Jessup to stop interfering with the case if he was to get his proof.

Nick Storie could control his temper exactly, when necessary. This was one time he wanted to throw a real scare into someone. Exposure of the threatened type would do it.

Jessup's cases *would* all be overturned if it was shown he used the methods he *did* use. He would be discredited, and he would be through in his powerful little job. It should make Jessup pull in his horns enough, unless Jessup felt killing Sylvia to get Pancho off the streets was a means that would be justified by an end.

Nick didn't like Jessup. Not even a little. He never liked a person he couldn't trust, and Jessup's own mother would be a fool to trust him.

Why were there so many of his type in those positions? What lack in the system allowed it?

Nick drove directly down to Pancho's home in Boca Raton from Jessup's office. He found it easy to lose the tails – the easy one and the clever one – who were seen following him. They'd both be looking for him up toward Lauderdale about now.

He'd timed going onto the freeway just right to make them have to wait for two semis to pass. By then, he'd dropped back off on the other side of the cloverleaf. He then went into a filling station to fill the rental car, but didn't seem to be watched, so he went into another agency of the rental company and complained about the car balking at traffic lights so they gave him another one of a different model and color.

Next he stopped at a drive-in a short distance from the rental lot, but no one came, so they hadn't had time to put a locator beacon on it.

He went to A1A and south, then on a little-used secondary road to the interstate. He wasn't followed.

Now, here he was!

"Where was the car when it blew?" Nick asked Ed Murray, a sort of accountant or something who worked for Pancho.

"At her condo in Miami. She was coming over here, got in, turned on the ignition, and that was it."

"Do they have enough of the device to identify?"

"You'll have to ask them. It's a stinking lousy setup! The jefe was going to marry her! He didn't snuff her!"

"Who else might have done it and why? I think Pancho said you can talk to me."

"It doesn't make any sense. I mean, it was a way to get to Pancho. That's all! Nobody would have been after her!"

Nick thought a minute, then, "Who would want to get to Pancho who might do something like that?"

"I can't think of anyone. Not any of the mmajor crime families. It could start a war. They get along, and their sole supplies of certain commodities would be cut off, so it could only hurt them. It doesn't make any sense that way, either.

"You know him. Everybody likes him. Even you, and you're a cop."

Nick nodded. It didn't make sense to him, either.

He headed back to Miami after a little while.

"What do you have on the detonator?" Nick asked Blaine.

"It was a couple sticks of dynamite," Blaine said. "Cap was wired to the starter wire."

"Then it went the first time she used the car after it was put on?"

"Uh-huh."

"Where did the tip come from?" He knew the police line had an automatic trace device on it.

"Payphone in the main lobby of the DuPont Plaza hotel. There are several in a row. Nobody saw who made the call."

Nick could see several lines of approach. He was sure he could get Pancho out of jail very quickly, so he went to Sylvia's condo to get a feel of the case. There was a large burned spot on the pavement at her parking space.

He used the key Blaine gave him to get in. The place had been carefully searched. Probably at least twice, once by Blaine's men and once by Jessup's. Nothing major would have been missed.

A little innocuous item had helped a lot in another investigation a long time ago that he hoped would do the same here. He knew what he wanted wouldn't be left around by Jessup's crew if they found it, so he went to the refrigerator and into the vegetable bin, but there was no receipt stuck to anything.

Store receipts had the time and date on them.

Nick sighed and started to close the door, then yanked it open again to make a little smirk. He'd seen exactly what he hoped would do it. An unopened carton of milk.

He read the code on the top. "Use before Feb. 19, 1993" in nice black letters.

The code was for one week on the shelf, so the milk was bought after the twelfth. Pancho was arrested on the day of her death, the fourteenth.

The milk was the brand carried by Publix Supermarkets. Nick found the super and asked if he knew how Sylvia got her groceries and when.

"She went after them, like anybody else."

"In her car?"

"Nah! She walked the two miles over to Publix!"

"She always traded at Publix?"

"Yeah. Most of 'em do here. It's closest and has a lot of sales."

"She went after her groceries Thursday or Friday?"

"I suppose. Sales run Thursday to Wednesday. She always went Thursday, because stuff's fresher the first day."

"Thanks! You can't know how much help you've been!" Nick said, heading for his car.

Chapter eleven

"That milk carton and the word of the manager of her condo destroys any evidence you have against DeGulio," Nick reported to the state's attorney, a John Galahue. "You have no case and never did and you know it."

"We have a tip that he was seen around the car," Galahue said stubbornly. "His prints were all over it!"

"It was his car," Nick said as stubbornly. "He rode in it and even drove it a lot. Certainly his prints were in it! DeGulio wouldn't leave his fingerprints anywhere they could even vaguely incriminate him!

"Your anonymous tipster saw him around that car?

"When?"

"Thursday afternoon."

"He was on his boat with several other people from before noon Thursday until after noon Friday. So much for your *alleged* tipster! She used the car Thursday. No bomb was on it then!

"So! What's all this?"

"DEA wants him held."

"So? DEA runs your office? Would you like the public to know you hold people on charges you know are phony on instructions from the DEA? Really?"

"You wouldn't do that! He's a known drug supplier!"

"Then charge him with that. I'll say to you exactly what I said to that crooked Jessup bastard! You took an oath to uphold the law! You, in addition, are an officer of the court!

"You're a perjurer of that oath from the moment you knew those charges were false, making you no better than Jessup *or* DeGulio! The people out there have lost all faith in the police and courts because of people like *you*!

"You turn him loose. Now! – or I start some publicity you'll never live down! Your political career is over from that moment!"

Nick slammed out of the office.

Now to see who ran for cover! He didn't believe for one second Jessup had killed her or had done anything other than seize an opportunity, but it still amounted to his aiding and abetting the real killer.

"Nick?" Blaine asked when he went into the station two hours later. "What in the hell have you stirred up? Why in hell did you threaten Galahue?"

"Threaten? What are you talking about? I told him if he didn't release DeGulio after I took him proof the charges are false his political career's over. I'll go public with it."

"I have a warrant from his office. I'm ordered to arrest you on charges of interfering with a felony case in progress and for obstruction of justice. It's a legal warrant, and I have to serve it."

"It's not a legal warrant and you damned well know it. Galahue had to lie to a judge to get that one, but I guess that doesn't affect your end of it.

"I get my phone call, right?"

"They can't do anything about that. Have you got an out?"

"I'm going to go public. Exactly like I said I would. I'm going to tie Galahue's crooked tail in a knot, then I'm going after Jessup. If we had his lousy type out of the DEA, they'd double their conviction rate and get a lot of those drugs off the streets. The theory that says they have to become as bad as the dealers themselves to catch them stinks! It's about time somebody said, `Enough!'

"I'm saying it!"

He picked up the phone and called Paddy. Paddy would be there the first flight. Nick could always depend on Paddy to support and aid his men – if they were in the right.

Blaine managed to keep Nick out of a cell until Paddy stormed in like a runaway mad bull. Nick finally calmed him down enough to explain Blaine had no choice in the matter, it was Galahue operating on orders from Jessup.

"We'll have to take this Jessup bastard down a notch or two, won't we?" Paddy said. "You have something or you wouldn't have called me. What?"

"You can demand and get what the court based the warrant on. I'm an officer in your department, so you'll naturally want to make an IA investigation.

"From what the warrant says and what Capt. Blaine tells me we can start a little housecleaning right away!"

Paddy talked with them for a few minutes more, then took the warrant to the issuing judge and demanded the evidence for review by Internal Affairs, Collier County Sheriff's Dept. He got a copy of a tape Galahue made in his office.

"He's a state's prosecuting attorney with a bugged office?" Paddy asked the judge. "Well! Does he inform his client's of that tidbit, or is he above such petty things as the law?"

He took the tape back to Blaine's office where they sat to listen to it. It was just what happened from when Nick came in until he mentioned the milk carton, which was excised.

Nick said just before that, "The evidence is far worse than flimsy in a couple of spots."

Galahue: "We have a tip that he was seen around the

car. His prints were all over it!"

Nick: "It was his car."

Galahue: "We also have an eyewitness to his being right there to rig the bomb."

Nick: "You turn him loose! Now!"

Galahue: "I can't do that! We've got him cold!"

Nick: "Now! – or I start some publicity you'll never live down!"

Galahue: "Detective Storie! I can't do that! What are you saying?"

Nick: "Your political career is over!"

Galahue: "I have to do what the courts order! They gave me the warrant and I was assigned the case!"

Nick: "Making you're no better than Jessup! You turn him loose!"

There were the sounds of Nick slamming out.

Paddy looked at Nick. "It's a pretty good job of splice, but the intonation's a bit off, and the inflection's exactly the same in both places you said to turn him loose."

"He had the DEA's help with doctoring the tape. I didn't trust Galahue for one second. He'd already gone too far, so I was wired when I went in. I'll get the recorder if Capt. Blaine will allow me to leave for a minute?"

"I suppose they wouldn't miss looking through the car since you've been here," Blaine said. "Did you figure on that?"

Nick grinned and went out. He went directly to the elevator and surprised the two women in it by lifting the emergency escape hatch and taking the recorder. He stayed in at the ground floor and rode back up to Blaine's office on the second floor. He'd been gone for exactly three minutes. Blaine shook his head.

Nick played the tape of his visit to Galahue's office.

Blaine mentioned the quality of the little recorder and how clearly it picked up things.

"It's a thing made by Crane for the government," Paddy said. "It's accepted by the courts. It's impossible to splice a tape from it, and it's voicecoder quality all the way.

"Shall we go have a talk with the judge who issued the warrant?"

Blaine grinned and told his secretary they would be gone most of the rest of the afternoon.

"Do I have to say I authorized the wire?" Blaine asked Paddy. "I won't, you know."

"I did that," Paddy replied. "Nick pointed out that Jessup was crooked from his prior trip here, which was why I arranged for him to come this time. All my officers have authorization to use our special equipment at any time they feel any law officer in *any* department *any*where is exceeding authority. That is up to and including my own offices."

Which was true, but it hadn't been discussed before Nick left Naples. Paddy was like that. He wouldn't lie, but he'd already established rules to fit what he felt were reasonable situations.

The judge blustered around a bit, then took them back to her chambers to hear the tape after checking on the Crane machine and finding it was, indeed, precisely what Paddy represented it as being. There was a cyclical ultrasound wave on the tape as it was recorded. It recycled every time the recorder was stopped and wouldn't match if the tape were spliced.

The judge listened through one playing and dropped the machine into her desk drawer, then used the phone to order Galahue to come to her private chambers.

Immediately.

Galahue's tape was in the recorder on her desk when he came in. He nodded shortly to Blaine, looked quizzically toward Paddy, and smirked at Nick.

"Mr. Galahue, Lt. Storie claims that the tape you presented to this office is altered," Judge Vickers said. "You presented the tape to me to obtain a warrant for the detention of Lt. Storie after swearing an oath as to there *not* being any tampering with the tape.

"Do you here renew that sworn oath?"

Galahue looked a little worried, but repeated the oath.

Judge Vickers played Galahue's tape and had him say it was the one he'd presented without any alterations.

She then took the Crane voicecoder from her drawer and placed it on the desk beside the one with Galahue's tape in it. Galahue turned a sickly grey color and began to sweat.

"Where did you get a Crane coder?!" Galahue asked.

"The owner of Crane International lives in our area," Paddy answered. "He donates lots of equipment to our department."

"You were unaware Lt. Storie was wired, but that's all right," Judge Vickers said easily. "Lt. Storie wasn't aware your office was bugged.

"A little oversight, Mr. Galahue. The law requires you tell people there is a recording being made unless it's in plain view. You've prosecuted people for violating that law in this courtroom at least twice.

"Do I have to play the real tape for you or do you understand the charges I'm entering against you?

"I'm sure you're aware of your rights, but I'll be happy to repeat them for you, should you so require?"

Galahue dropped down into his seat and clammed.

"That's you!" Nick said. "I said I'd destroy you!"

"Now, Nick!" Paddy said happily, "You still have to hang that Jessup character out to dry!"

"I hereby vacate the warrants against Lt. Nathaniel Storie and Francisco DeGulio and issue in their stead warrant against John Sean Galahue for obstruction of justice, false imprisonment, and malfeasance in the act of perjury!" Judge Vickers said sternly. "Lt. Storie, Capt. James, the court apologizes to you for the extreme inconveniences, but thanks you both for exposing this disgusting perversion of justice within our bailiwick.

"I'll call the bailiff for our Mr. Galahue.

"Lt. Storie, may I assume you *will* be available for testimony against Mr. Galahue, should he be so foolish as to not plead nolo contendre?"

They chatted for a few minutes more. The bailiffs came to get Galahue, who asked that Judge Vickers set bond.

She replied sternly, "One million dollars. We'll take consignment of assets, but you are *not* skipping out on this!"

He looked terribly sick to Nick as he was led out.

Nick, Blaine, and Paddy headed back to Blaine's office.

"Well, Nick! How's the case coming?" Paddy asked.

"It's not doing very well, but maybe Pancho can give me a lead or two. There has to be something."

"He'll handle it," Blaine said. "It's going to be bloody, I'm afraid, but that's the kind of people who get into this sort of thing."

"No. He'll let me handle it. He said he would."

"One thing I can say – well, two – about Mr. DeGulio!" Blaine said. "If he says it, it's what he said, as he said it. He'll also stop problems from the druggies against my department so long as we play by the rules."

"He always plays by the rules," Paddy said. "It's what scares me most about him. It's a game."

"Only on one level," Blaine said. "On another, it's deadly serious to him.

"We'll stop by the cells and let him out. You'll meet him.

"He's in a tight spot. His people have been viciously held down and almost destroyed by sordid little dictators for most of their history. He's found a way to let them get a few things and some power. He's very strong on helping his people."

"There have to be other ways," Paddy protested.

"Yeah? Like what?" Nick asked. "Our own lovely government insists on shoring up the government they have now no matter how violently it represses the people. We get copper from them or something, so they can't be touched. We deny knowing about the obvious corruption of the ruling party.

"You tell me one thing they can do. What else is there?"

"Nick...," Paddy started, then shrugged.

"We could spend about ten percent of what we're spending on chasing the drug dealers and suppliers on building a decent economy for those people and there wouldn't be much of a drug trade," Blaine agreed. "We like to cry and moan about the DeGulios of this world, but they're our own creation.

"You're going to like DeGulio, Paddy. Everyone does! He's naturally a charming person"

"Not Jessup!" Nick shot back. "Not Galahue!"

"And look what *they* are!" Blaine smiled. "You told me right from the first that Jessup had no honor, but DeGulio does.

"Galahue has no honor. That type won't like anyone who shows any great code of integrity, because they can't understand them.

"Jessup likes to throw his weight around. Power and money are the two things that have any meaning to him at all, and DeGulio has both, so he envies and hates him.

"I'll do everything I can to stop DeGulio or anyone else from bringing dope into this country. It's something we have to do or our way of life is at risk. That doesn't mean I don't like, understand, and even respect the man. I do."

They went into the holding area. Galahue was being led in from booking as DeGulio came out from property. Galahue was beaten and scared. DeGulio was calm and beaming. He embraced Nick and seemed genuinely pleased to meet Paddy.

"I knew you'd get me out, Nickie!" DeGulio smiled. "You see, I have every faith in my friends."

Galahue spat an obscenity. Paddy couldn't help but notice the sharp contrast in the two. "What are we becoming?" he asked of no one.

Chapter twelve

"Well, Nickie! It seems you *have* come to visit me at my home again!"

Nick had driven Pancho down to his place in Boca Raton from the jail. Paddy's plane didn't leave for four more hours, so he came along.

"Capt. James, you haven't ever been here before. Just do as you please and go where you like. We're informal.

"Mi casa es su casa."

"You live well," Paddy replied, looking around the place.

Paddy, as everyone predicted, *did* like Pancho. "Please call me Paddy. Everybody does."

"Ah? There is censure in your tone?" Pancho smiled.

"It's only that all these people tell me how you do what you do for your people back home, This seems to tell a different story."

Pancho laughed. "I see! It is the double standard, no? It is fine with you that the head of the Red Cross lives in a large mansion that puts the White House to shame, has chauffeurs and private planes, and has all expenses paid – in addition to an obscene salary and that your own politicians live in ostentatious luxury, voting themselves ridiculous wages, but I should live in a hovel?

"Why? Because I'm not North American?"

Paddy grinned. "Touché. You certainly destroyed any argument I could hope to make, didn't you?"

"Have a drink, Paddy! The bar is excellent, as you will find. Nickie, I declare you off duty for one hour.

"It helps to have a small libation while I've contrived to keep you from your new bride so cruelly. You like Cuervo Gold, I believe?

"If you would be so kind as to pour me a small glass of Scots Whiskey and soda on the rocks, I simply *must* take a fast shower and get out of these stale garments. No one will be around. Ed should arrive as soon as he learns I am no longer incarcerated.

"I know Nickie wants to speak with me, so I will make haste."

"There are no servants?" Paddy asked.

"*Not* here!" Pancho replied hotly, then continued, "Paddy, I must apologize. You couldn't understand, but my parents were servants, as was I as a youth.

"People come here because they want to be here. They do for themselves and clean up after themselves unless there is a party where I hire people who ask for the work.

"It is one of the reasons I was going to marry Sylvia. She is ... was an excellent cook, and liked housework.

"I have my own double standard, you see. No servants, but a wife's place is taking care of the home."

He stopped, and his eyes clouded over, then he said, very quietly, "Nickie, I do not believe in revenge or cruelty. I have seen far too much of that.

"We will find who has done this. I will exact repayment with excessive interest. This I promise you."

"It was Jessup and that crooked lawyer who had you locked up. The lawyer's going to get his from the courts. I don't think it would be smart to go after Jessup in any personal way."

"Nickie, I don't care about that part of it. I am used to much worse jails than you dream of in your most horrible nightmares. Jessup will be destroyed in his career for this. I will see to it. He isn't of any consequence.

"I want the one who did that to Sylvie!" He went into a hall and away.

Paddy exclaimed at the bar and went around to mix

them all drinks. He knew Nick liked tequila and grape-fruit juice, tall, with lots of ice. Paddy seldom drank, but made himself a weak vodka Collins. He then poured Pancho a shot of twelve year old Scotch over ice and shot in an equal amount of soda.

"I think maybe Francisco DeGulio is probably the most decent man I've ever met," Paddy finally said. "How can he be mixed up in this drug business?"

"I'd say because there simply isn't anything else available. He tries to keep it away from the average Joe, but it's our own scum who peddle it to their own people.

"I also think the local drug scene would be ten times more violent and would affect ten times as many people as it does if he wasn't who he is.

"Paddy, the ones who control the drugs up north are greedy US citizens. Kids are killing each other. They're cruising around in cars, shooting randomly!

"It's not that bad down here. It should be a hell of a lot worse, considering how much of the illegal stuff comes through here."

"It's more an extremely frustrated overpopulation. I know you're not trying to excuse Pancho, but you sound like you are."

"Who's excusing whom for what?" Ed Murray said, coming in from the unlocked garden door. "Call me Ed. I've seen Nick before. You are?"

"This is Paddy James," Nick introduced.

"Ah! Captain James! Here to help Nick look for clues?

"I think El Jefe will handle things when he's out. They can't hold him too much longer on those phony charges, but I'll never understand why he refuses to let me get a good lawyer to tie that Jessup bastard's ass in a knot!

"You know what he told me? He said Nickie would get him out at the proper time, and without making an unnecessary fuss! Can you believe that?"

"Nickie did," Paddy replied dryly. "Pancho's taking a shower."

Ed went behind the bar, shaking his head. "Why is he *always* right? I should have known! That Scotch and soda should have told me. You've got your drinks and it's there."

They chatted awhile about various incidental things, then Pancho came in for his drink. He joined the conversation. Pancho finally asked Ed to drive Paddy to the airport and to see him safely off, and told Nick to follow him into the kitchen. They could see what was there to throw together for supper while they discussed other things.

Word was out that El Jefe was no longer in the pen, so people started dropping in. There was a mix of hoods and higher class normal citizens and business people. There didn't seem to be any locked doors. People brought food with them or rummaged around in the kitchen the same as Pancho and Nick were doing. Pancho asked Nick if he liked lobster. Nick said he most definitely did, and Pancho went into a walk-in freezer to bring out a couple of large tails. That started Nick thinking about lobster and freezers.

Pancho was an excellent chef. He'd been a cook as a youth (Not so long ago. He was just thirty two now.), and made a fat loaf with the lobster, wrapped it in a pastry-like crust, and made a delicious thick white wine sauce to pour lightly over it. He fried sliced cauliflower, broccoli, mushrooms, onion, celery, and munster cheese in hot garlic butter for a side dish. The salad was cold lettuce, cherries, pineapple, and small bits of sharp cheddar cheese with a mayonnaise-based dressing. It was as good as any meal he'd ever eaten in any fine restaurant! Better!

"One does what one must in this life," Pancho said, glowing when Nick complimented him on the food.

Over coffee with a touch of fine cognac and German apple pie Pancho finally sat back and said it was time to get down to business.

"Nickie, earlier, in the kitchen you were thoughtful. Something has occurred to you."

"I was just wondering if Lanier has the connections to have the bombing done. He's the type of halfassed idiot who would consider it your fault he was caught in his own little murder. He's also the type who would do something like that to get at you. He's not smart."

"Lanier? I think no one would be stupid enough to do that kind of thing for him."

Nick shook his head. "I can't think of anyone else, so you'll have to give me a clue. As you say, nobody would be stupid enough to attack you or your friends for any amount of money.

"*Could* it be one of the families?"

"Why would they hurt Sylvie? That would only start a war they couldn't hope to win.

"No. They aren't that stupid when it comes to certain kinds of things. Supplies of the product would end should I become angered with them. It would adversely affect their cash flow, so they would avoid such actions at all costs. They are driven by greed and all else is secondary to them.

"I know of no one who would wish to harm Sylvie directly. No one. There is no one who would try to harm Sylvie to anger me. No one is that stupid! Surely!"

"We're back to Lanier. He *is* that stupid."

"Ah! But no one is stupid enough to do such a thing in

his stead. He remains in jail awaiting trial.

"This means what I am seeing and hearing is merely a terrible dream!

"Oh, Nickie! How I wish to awaken!"

"Jefe, if no one would do such a thing for any reason except one person and no one would do it for that person for any reason, yet that thing was done, it was done by that person. Now that person is supposedly in a place, a position, from which it wasn't possible for him to do it, yet it was done. Therefore, that person was *not* where that person was supposed to be. That person did it."

"There is no way that person could have evaded ... no! You are thinking what you must be thinking! There is one single way, one single other person who could cause that one person to *not* be where he could do no such thing!

"Nickie, if what must be true *is* true it exceeds any promises I made. There were limits on those promises and you know it."

"I'll have to go back to Naples to find if there was any deal made. Just give me some time to check it out, Pancho."

"You can check one thing now. If he did any such thing he knows you will figure it out, so he will be gone."

Nick nodded and went to the phone. He dialed Jessup's number. It rang fifteen times before he hung up.

"That number was supposed to reach him at any time," Nick said through his teeth. "He's skipped.

"Pancho, I don't believe he'd do anything that extreme. Not deliberately. I really don't!

"Don't go after him until we know. Please!"

"Nickie, I will promise you I will not do anything to Jessup unless and until it is shown, as the court would say, by the preponderance of the evidence that he had a direct connection with Sylvie's death – which includes his knowing Lanier would do such a thing. That includes only the area within the United States of America and its possessions. If he is not any longer here he is not in the jurisdiction of any promises.

"I have made *no* promises about Lanier should he, indeed, have been free to do such a thing. I refuse to make any such promises now.

"Fair enough?

"It means you must get to him before I do. If you can get a definite conviction without him getting free to do anything else such, you may handle it. If some filthy vermin such as Jessup can again have him released there is no promise of anything.

"If judges would allow no such stupid deals for proven violent criminals people would not be forced to act against their natures to settle such matters themselves."

"You understand what my argument would be now?"

"Nickie, if it wasn't the drug it would be something else. I supply a product to people here who do with it as they may.

"Again, they take the stuff knowing full well what it can do. They assume all responsibility for their actions at the first moment they use it. Perhaps I will not properly be able to listen to your remonstrations of addiction and excuse, but you also will not hear that those refuse have chosen the life of addiction.

"I won't hear of how they didn't believe it would ever happen to them. All they have to do is read a newspaper or look around at their own communities and they *know* better! It is what they have *chosen* to do! Your arguments to the contrary do not make sense and you know it. The spillover into other communities is only because you have allowed a system to evolve that concentrates on the rights and privileges of the criminal while recognizing no rights of victims of those criminals. If you will look at your system of so-called justice from outside and in pure logic you must note your society is insane.

"You're a police officer. What happens if you irresponsibly cause the death of an innocent person? Will you be suspended for a month with pay? Is that not a *reward* for your actions? If a policeman is found guilty of a crime, which almost never happens when only you investigate yourselves, is he sentenced as severely as the normal citizen?

"You know he is not.

"If a politician commits a crime, is HE treated as a servant or is he treated as a normal citizen or is he given no more than a token sentence when he is sentenced at all?

"This society is totally corrupt and you know it. You have allowed something to happen that people even so far back as Plato warned against: You have allowed lawyers to dictate laws, first, then to control everything else through considerations of those laws. Almost all your politicians are lawyers. All the judges are lawyers. No corporation dares to move without approval by its lawyers. People are finding impossible reasons to have lawyers sue other people. Even the medical profession is now controlled by lawyers. They have inserted themselves into every small aspect of our lives. They have developed and inserted an exclusive language – and I use the term 'exclusive' very deliberately – of their own and a system of rules of their own and have set themselves up as de facto rulers of everything.

"Now they want a world court. That is the end of

freedom for anyone, anywhere.

"Nickie, I am preaching on my soapbox. My country is held in thrall by a petty little egocentric dictator, though they call him El Presidente. He was selected by the people in a free vote you will say, but the only people who may be selected for any office are people the *lawyers* say are qualified.

"Now! I fight against lawyers there and I will fight against them here. I will not again so show from what deep recesses of thought my actions are drawn, but you are my friend, and I have no secrets from my friends.

"If Lanier was free to kill my Sylvie I am going to kill him. I am going first to torture him beyond anything of which you can conceive, then I will kill him. If it eventuates that your Mr. Jessup was aware such a thing might happen he will meet the same fate, though not necessarily by my hands. It will not be a thing placed into the hands of lawyers."

Nick nodded. He wasn't surprised by any of it, only at the intensity of Pancho's emotions. If Lanier was out he wanted to find him – if simply to prevent having Pancho become what he so detested. He wasn't a vengeful or violent person. Nick didn't want him to become one.

<u>*Chapter thirteen*</u>

"Let me get this straight!" Paddy demanded, red-faced. "You say this Jessup asshole managed to get Lanier out of jail here and he murdered that girl?"

"That's the way I figure it. Nothing else makes much sense. No one else would be stupid enough to try anything like that. Anyone who wanted to get to Pancho would go after him directly – and no one's that stupid, either.

"It's easy to check. Jessup's already gone."

Marsha picked up the phone and dialed, waited, gave her name, and said it's official business and urgent, then hung up.

"She's in court. She'll recess and call me."

They waited about ten minutes until the phone lit up, then Marsha said, "Margaret? I had to call you because there's some sort of mixup at holding and they suddenly can't find Lanier.

"What's going on?"

She listened a minute, then said, "Listen, Mar. I'll tell you what we have, then you decide if you're going to let the feds run your court for you ... It's not that. You know me better than that ... Mar, get off the high horse, and listen to me!"

She grinned and shrugged at Paddy and Nick, waited a few more seconds, then said, "If you're through, let me say something, okay?

"What we figure happened is a DEA agent by the name of Jessup made some kind of deal ... Let me finish!"

She shook her head and waited, then, "If you're through I'll go on. I'm not interfering with your court. The feds did that ... What?"

She put her hand over the mouthpiece and said,

"Margaret had already figured something would go wrong. She's feeling guilty before she finds out what it is. She'll run down ... (Back into the phone). Are you going to listen now?

"Mar, we think Jessup made a deal to use him as a DEA informer or something, but he's killed a girl in Miami ... Let me finish, Mar. We have to know, because it's altogether too possible Jessup knew he'd do something like that. He wanted ... Yes. Exactly. I'll let you talk to Paddy." She handed him the phone. Nick and Marsha went out to the coffee urn while Paddy talked to Judge Collins.

Nick said, "She let him go?"

"The feds came in and insisted it was a done deal. They went over her head and she was already mad as hell about it. What's bothering her is that she didn't go over *their* heads and demand they stay the hell out of her business."

Paddy came in and waved at Nick to follow him. He told Marsha to bring a voicecoder and to come along. His face was set in its most furious frame, so neither said anything. They just followed him.

Paddy was generally the easiest-going person in Naples. Nick had seen that set of features once before when a child molester had been released without having to serve time and the department hadn't been notified so they could watch him. That one ended up at homicide because the parolee had killed two little eight year old girls.

Tiny Menthorne was just coming in. He saw the look on Paddy's face and stepped aside without comment. Nobody was stupid enough get in Paddy James' way when he was as furious as he obviously was.

Paddy went directly to a cruiser, got in, and was

started off before Marsha and Nick were in and settled. He used the lights and siren, but drove within the posted speed limit directly to the federal building. There was a courier on the steps with an envelope, which Paddy took without breaking stride or saying a word.

They went to the third floor without one word passing among them. Paddy slammed open the door and marched toward the back. Several people started to say something, saw his face, and backed off.

There was a big mahogany desk in front of and beside a door with "Director" in black block letters on the frosted glass. A secretary sitting there stood and said, "You can't...!" just as Paddy reached the door.

It was locked. Paddy lifted his foot and kicked the door below the knob. The whole side of the door splintered.

Marsha snapped on the recorder and grinned weakly at Nick.

There were two people sitting across the desk from a third. Paddy simply snarled, "You two were leaving!" He stared hard into the eyes of the man sitting behind the desk, frozen in shock and more than a little fear.

"Federal Drug Enforcement Agency Sub-Director Harold Francis Colton, I hereby place you under felony arrest on the charges of accessory to murder one, impeding the courts, obstruction of justice, intimidation of witnesses, conspiracy to commit murder, and any other charges that may crop up!" Paddy said evenly. "You have the right to remain silent. Should you give up that right, anything you say can and will be used in a court of law against you. You have the right to an attorney. If you cannot afford one, the courts will appoint one to represent you.

"Do you understand these rights?"

"What the hell! What's going on?" Colton cried.

"*Do* you understand these damned civil rights you have denied to others?"

"What is this? GET OUT!"

"Cuff him!" Paddy demanded of Nick, who didn't dare to pause. Colton reached out to push at Nick and found himself staring down the barrel of Paddy's army issue .45. He froze. Nick cuffed him.

Colton started to say something and Paddy shoved the envelope he'd received on the steps into his mouth. "That's the warrant! Take him to the cruiser and lock him in the cage, Lt. Storie! Right the hell NOW!"

It was going to be a very tight fit riding back to the station with the three of them in the front seat, but nobody dared to argue.

Judge Collins was waiting in her chambers when they marched Colton ungently in and shoved him into a chair across her desk. She stared at him for a full minute in silence, then ordered, "Capt. James, you may remove the handcuffs.

"Mr. Colton, you sat right there a few days ago and took full personal responsibility for any illegal acts committed by your Mr. Lanier after this court released him into your custody.

"He has, we now have strong evidence, committed at least one murder.

"That is one charge on the warrant that Capt. James delivered to you when you were taken into custody. That we also have very strong evidence you knew that act or something much like it would be committed results in the further charges.

"I will *not* permit any such as you to use my court in such a manner! Not by you and not by anyone up to and including the Chief Justice of the Supreme Court!

"You will produce Mr. Lanier – immediately! – or you will be formally charged as accessory to murder in the first degree. In addition you will further be charged with criminal conspiracy with Agent Jessup of the Miami branch should you not produce Mr. Jessup and should Mr. Jessup's testimony not absolve you.

"There will be no further discussion of any of this until Mr. Lanier and Mr. Jessup are before me, is that clear?"

Colton decided to pull his arrogant "Federal Agent" act. It didn't impress Judge Collins at all, so he demanded the use of a telephone. Collins pointed to the one on her desk and said, "One call. Local."

Colton called the state's attorney's office, talked for about two minutes to arrange for a lawyer, then hung up and started to punch another number. Collins placed her index finger onto the receiver button, and said, "One."

"Let him make one more," Paddy said. "It will show them how serious we are."

Colton then punched another number from memory, quickly explained what had happened, and looked up to Judge Collins. "What's the bail?"

"As Agent Jessup already seems to be missing and this is a capital matter, bail is denied."

"You can't do that to *me*! I'm an official agent of the US federal government!"

"I just did! Your time is up! Finish your call!"

"Send someone over here to get me out of here!" Colton demanded of the phone. "These yokels can't arrest a federal agent!"

Judge Collins took the receiver to say, "Consider the probable publicity before you stick your neck into that noose! I will *not* drop or alter charges. Federal agents are not above the law here, and this is capital murder!" She slammed down the phone and yelled, "Bailiffs! In here! Now!"

Two bailiffs ran into the room. She pointed toward Colton and ordered, "Book him! Here's the warrant and charges. Let them know down there beyond doubt that no court or judge takes precedence over this court's charges until such time as they are resolved to *my* satisfaction! Turn this one loose for *any* reason and I'll put the ones who do it away for contempt – where only I can release them!

"Get this slime out of my chambers and send in the fumigators! I'll play hell getting the stench of him out of here!"

Colton was led out.

"Can you believe that ass?" Collins demanded. "Can't arrest him because he's a federal agent? Don't they even screen *directors* over there? Where do they *find* these people?

"Marsha, don't you say one damned word to me about how stupid I've been to let them manipulate me in the first place! I *know* it!

"I don't remember ever being this angry in my life! The gall of that slimeball! I'll hang that arrogant bastard by his ba...!

"Okay. I'm calming down now.

"What next?"

"We have to get our hands on Lanier before DeGulio does," Nick said. "He promised to give me some time, but not much.

"I want Jessup. Colton's there to be the stooge for his little scheme if it backfires, which it damned well did! It's planned to be handled quietly and interdepartmentally.

"Judge Collins, I don't really believe Jessup meant for Miss Perez or anyone else to get hurt. He only meant for

Lanier to get him some way to tie DeGulio up for him. He's obsessed with DeGulio."

"To tell you the truth, he used the argument that you have been accepting valuable presents from DeGulio in getting Lanier released from confinement," Collins replied. "Tell me what's going on there."

"Pancho and I are friends. It was just something that happened. We like and respect each other.

"He gave me a little place on Martinique he can't use anymore for my wedding present. There are no strings attached of any kind whatever, and never could be.

"If Jessup or anyone else can get evidence on Pancho to tag him for anything he's done I won't lift a finger. He knows that. He won't ever interfere with my business and I won't interfere with his."

"You are a police officer."

"I'm a homicide cop in Naples, Florida. The only thing that ties me to this is a murder that Pancho had nothing to do with. He was going to marry Sylvia Perez.

"What he'll do to Lanier and maybe Jessup is something I don't want to think about. He may simply let it be known that he would consider it a favor if someone were to kill Jessup very slowly and painfully. He'd consider it a kind of poetic justice to do that, because Jessup set this thing up that resulted in Sylvia's murder. Lanier already told me all Pancho has to do is say that something someone did had displeased him, and that person was as good as dead and buried.

"Because of our friendship he'll let me handle Lanier if I can. If not, he'll handle that one personally, but not anywhere within my or the US courts' jurisdictions."

"I've heard very mixed things about Mr. DeGulio. Only Jessup and the DEA bunch and a few in the state attorney's offices have had much to say against him in any personal sense.

"Is it true he plays strictly by the rules and that every-one knows exactly what those rules are?"

"Ask Capt. Blaine in Miami," Paddy suggested. "Only the DEA agents and the attorneys for the state seem to play outside of any supposedly established rules.

"I met DeGulio and liked him. I can understand his point of view if I don't agree with it. Part of it."

"Aren't we supposed to find Lanier?" Marsha asked. "Isn't good old Federal Bigshot Colton our way to that?"

"We'll have to wait until he exhausts his big-shot fed pals," Collins said. "When he discovers I can and will hold him and that I can and will bring him to trial on those charges he'll try to deal."

"No deals!" Paddy snapped. "Not that one!"

"I agree," Nick said, thinking. "His only deal is to give us Lanier and for Lanier to convince us there wasn't any kind of conspiracy to kill anyone. Lanier will certainly try to cover his own tailfeathers, so Agent Jessup's his only other hope.

"I can get to Jessup. He really does think the govern-ment will get him out of trouble, no matter what."

"Then we'll put all this on hold and I'll get back to my dull courtroom," Collins said. "Dinner tonight, Marsh?"

"Uh-huh. We're having crab gumbo from Nick's recipe, but Nick ain't invited. He should spend a little time with his new bride."

That was too true! Nick grinned and waved, then headed out.

"Nickie! I've taken the liberty of sneaking away from Miami and the unpleasantnesses there," Pancho greeted as Nick entered his home. Janet had a hot delicious meal on the table very soon with Pancho's help.

Pancho swore he'd sneaked away and no one knew where he was.

Nickie, I won't stay here. They'll think of looking for me at your place, for one thing. For another, you and Janet want some privacy.

"I think maybe this isn't what we think. I also think you are in great danger personally, so want you to promise me you'll take the greatest care."

"I called Lonnie," Janet said. "No one would suspect Pancho would be there. Lonnie's going to stop by a little later on his way home and Pancho can go to his place with him.

"I think they'll get along great!"

"After supper I'll tell you what we have and what we think," Nick said. "I may need some help in locating Friend Lanier."

"There's a watch out for him," Pancho replied. "If he surfaces anywhere we'll tag him for you.

"Jessup's in Tampa."

"I think Jessup's going to have to come here to get Colton out of Judge Collin's jail. I'll tell you about it later while we wait for Lonnie."

They had the meal and talked for about two hours, then Lonnie stopped by. He and Pancho hit it off very well, arguing good-naturedly about a lot of things. Then Lonnie and Pancho left and Nick finally had some time for Janet – which he took immediate advantage of.

Chapter fourteen

"They can't locate Lanier, and we don't know where Jessup is," Paddy announced. "It seems there's some drug syndicate that wants to get him, so they're hiding him.

"Colton is *very* unhappy about that."

"DEA should be able to tell us where Jessup's hiding out, but they refuse to say anything other than that he's no longer in Miami and he's not in Collier County," Marsha added. "If we could find out where he is – if it's close – we could use it as a lever to pry something out of Colton."

"Let's go talk to Colton." Nick grinned. "Jessup's sorta close to here."

"You know where he is?" Paddy asked.

"Uh-huh," Nick replied. "I have my sources."

"Can't we get a statewide warrant from what we have on him?"

"I think so," Paddy answered. "If we can get one word out of Colton Collins'll give us the warrant."

Nick nodded, and they headed for the cells.

Paddy had Colton brought to a visitors' room. Nick had his little recorder sitting on the table. Colton took one look and shook his head.

"Just sit down and listen to what Nick has to say," Paddy asked. "Maybe you'll change your mind. I'll get coffee.

"Want a cup?"

"You've sure changed since yesterday's encounter," Colton replied, giving Paddy a confused and slightly speculative look. "I'll take a cup. Black."

Paddy went out. Nick grinned and said, "They're gonna let you twist in the wind, you know. You're the goat.

Jessup's in Tampa, but he's not going to say one word to give you an out. If he does he admits to things."

"No. The office told me he was out of the state. This isn't going to do you any good."

"My source doesn't lie to friends for expediency or to keep his branch from embarrassment. You might consider that.

"What has your office done for you, so far?"

Paddy brought in the coffee. Nick let the silence grow while he poured. Paddy was undecided where to perch, then worked his bulk into a chair.

Finally, Colton looked up and sneered, "The office is still investigating your charges. They'll give that Judge Bitch her orders and I'll walk!"

"Let's get something straight right now!" Paddy said evenly. "You make one more disparaging remark about Judge Collins – *or anyone else not in your own department* – and I'll see you rot in a cell with a few of the people *you* put there, got it?"

The look on Paddy's face made Colton back down.

"I'll definitely play this tape for Judge Collins," Nick said. "As to who can be described in any such terms, it was you and Jessup who went way outside the law to let a violent criminal out to kill an innocent woman.

"Get another little thing straight. You are accessory to murder for that. Those are state charges and entirely under the authority of the woman you just now called a bitch. Your oh so very powerful department *can't* give her orders.

"If they told you Jessup's out of state, they're lying to you. You know perfectly damned well they do that on a regular basis.

"We want Lanier and Jessup. If you're all we can get I have no problem with seeing you hung out to dry. If you give us one tiny fact Collins can have Jessup picked up and brought in. It'll then be your word against his.

"I would, personally, take yours. I know what Jessup is."

Colton sipped his coffee a minute. They all did.

"I'll tell you what," Colton said. "If Jessup's in Tampa, the office deliberately lied to me, which means they *will* let me take the heat. I know them.

"Like you said, they don't like publicity, so I'd be the easy way out.

"You prove he's in Tampa and I'll give you a tape or two of my own! You're not the only one who records everything!"

Nick nodded. He went to the end of the table and hid the keys as he punched for an outside line, then punched Lonnie's number.

"Micks residence," a voice answered.

"Isn't your host there? Why did you answer the phone? Is that smart?"

"Nickie! Lonnie has work to do, and no one would guess I'm here. I can see from your careful wording that others are present.

"What can I do for you?"

"I want you to tell Agent Colton where Jessup is being hidden at this moment."

"I see. It's beginning to dawn on his small mentality that his own department is going to allow him to take the fall alone. Your Agent Colton will know about my word. I will certainly cooperate with you!"

Nick put the phone set in front of Colton. "Francisco, `El Jefe,' DeGulio will tell you where Jessup is."

Colton looked at Nick, at the phone, at Paddy, at Marsha, and back to Nick. He took the receiver and said, "Uh, Mr. DeGulio?"

There was a short pause, then, "I have your word you will tell me the truth?"

Another pause. "If you give your word, everyone knows what you say is as good as written in stone. Where is he?"

He soon handed the phone back to Nick.

"Pancho? How do you like the area?"

"This place is as perfect as your own little island hideaway! Lonnie is a very charming and highly intelligent person. He well fits such a place. I think I will go with him tomorrow to work. There is much to learn from such a man.

"It is most refreshing to meet such a physically beautiful person who is also as spiritually and mentally beautiful!

"Janet said much about him, and I thought perhaps she was a bit stricken with him. When we first met last evening I immediately saw how any woman would be.

"He has no arrogance. He is a natural person who belongs with nature.

"Nickie, I first also thought this man must never meet the kinds of people I am generally forced to associate with, but they would affect him not one iota! I am at this very moment sitting on his log-railed porch. There is a mother deer with her colt standing not two feet from me begging for lettuce. There is a magnificent Great White Heron on the steps, also wishing tidbits. Birds and animals and beautiful gardens.... Janet said the women call him `Their Pan.'

"I think at times they are right. He could be a god!"

Nick laughed and said, "He affects most people like that. I have to go.

"No luck with Lanier?"

"No, Nickie. I will not call or check. They would find

from where I did so rather quickly. Be most careful, Nickie. Something occurs to me that frightens me about that one."

"I hope to have him in custody before the day's out," Nick said, then said his goodbyes and hung up to look at Colton.

"Well?"

"My god! I've spent six years trying to get something on El Jefe and he...," Colton started, then shook his head. "The tape's kept in my office with the rest of them. It's in a locked file cabinet. It's marked with the date. The combination to that file is left forty seven, right one fourteen, left two, right sixty six.

"I'll give you a written permission to get it. Mrs. Little – she's the one at the desk by the door – will give you all kinds of hell. I'll tell her you're after the evidence that'll clear this mess up. You have to swear to me you won't touch anything else in that file and that you'll leave it locked."

"Mr. Colton, I've had you brought here with these people for you to listen to and authenticate a tape recording Lt. Storie purports to recently have obtained from your office's private files with your written permission," Judge Collins announced. "None of us have yet heard the recording, but Paddy tells me it will convince me to issue a warrant for the apprehension of Agent Jessup.

"Do you state you are under no coercion?"

"I am under only the coercion of wishing to save my own as ... hide. I think the part that will interest you is coded on the outside, if I may see the tape label?"

Nick handed him the tape. Colton looked at the numbers written on the label and said, "Side B. Start at two hundred inches."

Nick snapped the tape into the machine and ran it to 200 on side B, then punched "Play":

There were six minutes of office chatter with some secretary about evidence in the photo files, then Mrs. Little announced Agent Jessup was there from Miami and wished to speak with him on a confidential department matter.

There was a two minute stretch of small talk, then, "We've got a way to get DeGulio, I think!" from Jessup.

Colton: "El Jefe? Right! I believe *that*!"

Jessup: "I'm serious! The hicks here have a punk in the pen who can give him to us on a platter – with a little incentive."

Colton: "A deal? What charges, and how strong?"

Jessup: "M one, but we can claim bias on the idiot cop who tagged him. It's a snap!"

Colton: "What kind of bias?"

Jessup: "Would you believe a cop who would take a gift of a vacation palace from DeGulio?"

Colton: "You're shitting me!"

Jessup: "Nah! He came to my office and I sent him right down to DeGulio's place. I figured if he had balls enough to walk in there claiming to be a local hick cop DeGulio would blow his stupid goddamned head off for him, but DeGulio thought it was cute or something and they got to be friends.

"The damned turdhead's on his honeymoon right now in the little palace El Jefe gave him for a wedding present!"

Colton: "Wonders never cease!

"This punk they tagged. He works for DeGulio?"

Jessup: "Better! He had some stuff that belonged to El Jefe. He didn't even know it.

"It's Lanier. From Chi and Motown. You're run across him. As stupid as that shithead cop who tagged him. Maybe worse.

"I can convince him DeGulio ratted him for the snuff. I can say DeGulio wanted him out of the way because he lost like four million bucks on the deal. Lanier's the type who'll get royally pissed about something like that."

Colton: "The Johns thing? It was that big?"

Jessup: "Unh-huh! They found a ton of the stuff in a freezer or something, and *Lanier* put it there, then some of it came up missing.

"I don't know the whole story and don't give a royal shit. All I need to know is that they got Lanier and the stuff and we can tie it around El Jefe's ass."

Colton: "Isn't Lanier more apt to try to gun DeGulio down than to info on him?"

Jessup: "I sincerely hope so! That'll solve the problem all the way around. We'll be rid of El Jefe either way — and he can't slip out of it from the morgue!"

Judge Collins slapped the "Off" button and yelled, "Bailiff!" She went to her desk, took a form from the top drawer, filled it out, handed it to her secretary for a stamp, then signed it. She handed it to the bailiff, who was waiting.

"Martin at state," she ordered. "Tell them Jessup's in Tampa, directly confirmed information. He's being hidden by the DEA in a direct coverup attempt. If he's not delivered here before the work day's over I'll put out warrants for the whole DEA and maybe for the US Attorney General, himself!

"Tell them you have inside information that I'll back off if he's delivered and they don't try anything stupid. Suggest then I won't overturn every conviction ever obtained through the Miami and Naples branches. Make it as plain I'll do that, minimum, if they bug me!"

The bailiff grinned, saluted her, and went out with the form.

Collins punched the "Play" button:

Colton: "Count me out! I'm not going to get into that bed!"

Jessup: "We're free and clear, no matter what! All we're doing is trying to set up an informant in the standard way. You do this kind of thing every day."

Colton: "Like hell I do!"

Jessup: "Oh? You don't make deals for information?"

Colton: "Not with some punk I know doesn't *have* any damned information!"

Jessup: "He can get it. Nobody else can.

"Look. This is the big one. We can get El Jefe. We'll have it made and can go right to the top on this thing.

"Do you know how long I've been after DeGulio? Years!"

Colton: "About six years. He's smart. I've thought I had him a couple of times, but he always has some out. Something I can't get past.

"The truth is, he's never in on the parts we can touch. He doesn't do anything himself, so we can't pin him. He comes out clean because, legally, he *is* clean. He's smarter than the bunch of us, and I don't kid myself about that."

Jessup: "That's what I'm saying! He keeps inside the legal thing for what we can prove. He's probably smart enough that he really doesn't do anything illegal himself, beyond stuff like getting Chico out before we can tag him. He's *there*, but doesn't actually do anything, at least not anywhere we have any jurisdiction.

"I'm determined to get him! He's been thumbing his nose at me for too long and I'm going to tag him – one way or another!

"Look! He's guilty as all hell and we both know it! This is our chance to tag the bastard!"

Colton: "What if Lanier only manages to get blown away himself with his normal stupidity?"

Jessup: "Then we're no worse off than right now, right? We'll save Florida the expense of housing him for the next twenty five years.

"All we have to do is get this Collins broad to release him in our custody, then we work the rest of it."

Colton: "But Judge Collins won't release him to go out of the county!"

Jessup: "So? These local hicks can't control where he goes once he's out. He disappears and we tell her he's under cover. He's right here, only in disguise. She's nothing but a local-yokel stupid broad. She's gullible as hell. She'll swallow it and sit around dreaming of what the publicity of catching DeGulio can do next time they're looking for a justice for the state supreme court.

"I've had plenty of lessons about using these hicks down here.

"Let's go make a deal!"

There were the sounds of scraping chairs, then of the office door closing.

"I see," Judge Collins said, dryly. "Maybe your Mr. Jessup will get another lesson about us hick local-yokels down here!"

Chapter fifteen

"No! You *will* have Agent Jessup standing here in this court by noon tomorrow or I *will* issue a warrant for the director of the DEA!" Judge Collins demanded of the phone. "I think perhaps I'm going to make a call to Washington right now, as a matter of fact. I don't think they have any idea what's going on down here.

"Incidentally, Mr. Franklin. UPI, ABC, NBC, CBS, CNN, TBS, and anyone else who cares to attend will be at that session when I issue that warrant. I will also enter the tape I informed you I was making of this conversation as containing supporting evidence of probable cause.

"Jessup will be standing before the bench by noon or that warrant will be issued at twelve oh one!

"Now good*bye*, Mr. Franklin."

She hung up and grinned across at Paddy, Nick, and Marsha. "That should light a few fires in a few hornets' nests!"

"My god, Marge!" Marsha cried. "Talk about a mixed metaphor!

"I suppose we should get back to the station now. Washington won't have a clue as to what's going on with Agent Jessup. That's one thing they don't dare allow to happen."

"What? You don't think Washington headquarters lets their agents pull this kind of disgusting crap?" Paddy asked sarcastically.

"It's not against what they'd allow if they thought they could get away with it," Marsha answered. "It's basically too dangerous *politically*, so they'll go into a panic if there's any strong chance of adverse publicity, so to speak.

"Marge will definitely demonstrate exactly how much

sand a hick local-yokel can put in their oil pan!"

"What? You have the *nerve* to criticize my mixed metaphors?" Collins demanded. "I don't even know where the hell you got half of that one!

"Get out of here! I'm due back in court forty minutes ago!

"Paddy, I'll see you tonight."

"You will?" Paddy looked surprised.

"Yup! My spouse and yours are dragging us to the ballet. We've *got* to stop meeting like that!"

They broke it up and left, everyone in a much lighter mood.

"I'm going to ride out to have a short chat with Pancho," Nick announced back at the station. "We'll have to figure where Lanier is. He can find him faster than we can."

"Nick, come into my office first. We have something important to discuss," Paddy said seriously. "You have to stay away from DeGulio, and you have to give back that place he gave you."

"No way José! I might've been in that position before we heard that tape, but not anymore!"

"What the hell do you mean? You're involving your-self with a known – all right. Suspected – felon!"

"Ah-uh!" Marsha replied. "Even the DEA, who's invol-ved closer than anyone, admitted he stays inside the law. They *suspect* he makes plans, but they don't have one piece of evidence that's true."

"He grows, processes, and distributes drugs!" Paddy insisted. "Everyone knows it!"

"Not very long ago everyone knew the world was flat," Marsha argued. "He's in Miami, so he's not growing anything. He's not processing it. He knows people who distribute drugs, but he certainly doesn't distribute them himself.

"He's a complete fraud! I have him figured!"

"I'll be double-dog damned!" Nick cried. "I wouldn't be the least bit surprised if you're right! He's conned the distributors, suppliers, processors, and those syndicate families!"

"What the bloody *Hell* are you talking about?" Paddy demanded.

"Paddy, all Pancho did was ... I have to talk to him! This is great!" Nick laughed. "He became the most powerful ... it's all on bluff and his personality! This is rich!"

"Well, *he* is!" Marsha laughed with Nick. "He was always so careful to not get involved with any violence. Even Capt. Blaine said he'd *stop* anything like that. Jessup, who's so obsessed with him, admits they simply have no evidence he's ever done anything outside the law. You can bet your last dollar Jessup checked him as close as anyone's ever been checked – and found absolutely *nothing*! After years of investigation they have nothing more than a few personal suspicions!"

"Jessup thinks Pancho's a lot smarter than he is – and he's damned well right about that!" Nick continued.

"Oh, for...!" Paddy exploded. "Nick, you go back to Boca Raton and ask him! He'll be honest with you. I guarantee him nobody in this department's going to give this one away!"

Paddy went back into his office shaking his head and giggling. Nick grinned at Marsha and said he was going visiting.

"Want me to get you a flight?" Marsha asked.

"No. Pancho's a guest. He had to get away from Raton for awhile.

"Marsh, we'll have to find Lanier. Pancho has a capacity for violence I don't ever want released. What Lanier did could do it."

She nodded seriously.

Nick went out to his car and started to get in. He noticed a greasy handprint on the chrome around the wheel well, started to get mad, then went cold.

He acted as though he were looking for something in the papers on the seat, then went back inside.

"Marsh! Paddy!" he called as soon as he was inside the office. "Have this area surrounded! Now! Get SWAT out here! *Fast*!"

"What?!" Paddy yelled, coming from his office.

"There's a greasy handprint on the left front wheel well of my car. It wasn't there when I parked it earlier."

Marsha called for all available units to surround the two-block area around the substation. They were to check everyone who came or went. Nick described Lanier to the radio.

Four minutes later he and two bomb squad cops went out to his car. One of them slid underneath.

"Two sticks of ... eighty percent," came from under the car. "Wired to the exciter wire. Hit the starter switch and there wouldn't be much of that car left to trace make and model.

"Hmmm. Disconnect the battery, Bob."

Nick snapped the hood latch. Bob took off the negative cable and said it was safe. Ralph, the one under the car, slid out a minute later with the dynamite and a detonator cap with some duct tape wrapped around them.

Nick grinned, and Bob reconnected the battery cable. Nick got in the car and headed for his place. He didn't expect them to get Lanier then – and they didn't.

"Hon, I want you to pack some things for a few days and go to your folks' place. I think he won't go after you, but you might ... I'll be damned!"

"What? You think ... that Perez woman! It was Pancho's car and Pancho rode in it all the time. Lanier thought he was at her place for some reason so he did that to get Pancho. It wasn't to set him up, it was to kill him."

"He probably checked and learned Pancho wasn't at the Boca Raton place, so figured he'd be there. The boat never occurred to him."

"Nick, he's dangerous! His being stupid makes him even *more* dangerous!"

Nick nodded.

They weren't followed to Sarasota, so Nick could be certain he wouldn't be followed back home. He went off the interstate at Alico Road and to Corkscrew on 41. There was no chance anyone was there, so he went on out to Lonnie's place.

There didn't seem to be anyone around, so Nick sat on the back porch to wait. Soon Pancho strolled in from the direction of the little pond behind the cypress swamp carrying two largemouthed bass and a fly rod. He grinned at Nick and announced, "Our supper. If I'd known you'd be here I'd have another, but these will be plenty.

"Having any luck on your own little fishing trip?"

"Some. Jessup'll be here before noon tomorrow. I'll want to talk with you about several things later, but for now I don't think Lanier planned to kill Sylvia. He was after you."

"I thought that was probable. It makes no difference. Nickie, this is a delightful place! I really haven't been so relaxed since I was on Martinique three years ago."

"It makes no difference?"

"No, Nickie, who he *meant* to kill doesn't matter. He killed Sylvie. He would have a far better chance of surviving had he been successful in killing me instead. He might be difficult to locate. He might be anywhere now.

"Perhaps Jessup will know."

"He's right here. Naples. He put a bomb in my car. Same thing as he used on Sylvia's car. He left a big greasy handprint on my wheel well. I took it off complete. It's four fingers and half the palm of his right hand.

"I suppose Paddy's thought it strange I didn't get the lab right on it, but I know who put it there and I have the print kit. I'll turn it in when I get back.

"I got a little scared that Lanier might do something to get me and would get Janet instead, so I took her up to her parents' place in Sarasota."

Pancho nodded and started cleaning the fish while they talked. He'd just finished the job and had them breaded and ready when Lonnie came in, so he dropped the fish into the skillet as soon as it was hot enough. He already had fresh asparagus simmered to perfection and on the plates, along with onion rings and zucchini fried in batter and a lettuce and cucumber salad.

The three chatted about various things. Pancho was going to work with Lonnie in the morning. He had a salt-and-pepper wig and a matching bushy moustache. He'd wear an old flannel shirt and overalls Lonnie had. No one would recognize him.

After dinner they moved outside to the little porch, but swarms of mosquitos drove them back inside.

"I'll have to get back to the station pretty soon now,"

Nick finally said. "I just wanted to ask you a few tiny questions, Pancho.

"Do you think you can get away with conning all those gangster types forever?"

Pancho exploded with laughter. He slapped Nick on the back and replied, "Yes!

"You see, it's too late for them to do anything about me now. I've become far too powerful."

"What is that about?" Lonnie asked. "What con?"

"Pancho came here with a story. He never had any connection with any drug cartel. He only convinced them he did. They let him set himself up as some kind of middle man. All he does is listen to what they're doing and nod wisely. He then collects his percentage and goes on his way."

"I have the connection back home. I know all the growers.

"You see, I was a servant in the home of a once very powerful political figure, who was the real processor. That man died. I was not involved in his death, but know who was. It was a member of my family.

"The man had long retired from politics, so far as anyone knew. He merely made statements or gave orders at odd times, always through *me*.

"I arranged with the persons who arranged his accident to hide the fact the man and his mistress were no longer among us and continued to give orders. I arranged that the monies coming in would be laundered in the US, then I would send the profits back home to the growers.

"I moved here out of necessity. A Mr. Alanza was importing the product and some very powerful people in the northeastern US were buying. I convinced Mr. Alanza of the wisdom of seeing that the product was not used in this area in any way, though he made some few deals on his own, as you are aware. It is where Mr. Lanier came into the equation.

"Mr. Johns, who you met recently, laundered the money for a time. Now it is two others.

"All I have ever done is give advice from time to time, such as the clever method Mr. Alanza used until very recently to bring the product into this country. I handled the funds – incidentally, I got forty percent – that I then passed back to my people. I also became a focal point for the attentions of your Mr. Jessup. He has spent several years almost exclusively in trying to find some way to, as he puts it, `Tag my ass!'

"Mr. Jessup was a poor choice for such a position. He allows personal irritations to dictate his actions. If I am receiving the full attention of the head of the agency in that area others receive very little, thus the operation continues, thus it is wasted.

"The Mr. Jessups of the world keep the Mr. Alanzas of the world in business.

"My value to them is more than the cost, Nickie. Without me to distract the DEA the operation would have been shut down four or five years ago.

"I have a certain value to your society in that I was eventually able to convince Mr. Alanza and others that violence is mostly counterproductive and basically very stupid.

"So! How did you know?"

"That was simple. Jessup spent several years investigating you almost exclusively and found nothing. With the resources under his control, that could only mean there wasn't anything to find. You were investigated more thoroughly than just about anyone, anytime, anywhere – and there was nothing.

"Do you think Alanza and the Donilettis will figure it

out now?"

"I suppose they already have." He smiled. "It makes no actual difference. My value is demonstrated.

"I will soon have to find another job, though. Without Jessup the equation changes radically. My people have enough to purchase all the land in the area in which they reside. They can now establish legitimate businesses there and can prosper.

"I have plenty to live very comfortably.

"You see, without a Jessup to distract, my value drops a very dangerous degree with those people. I can withdraw gracefully, and will tell them I must remain out of sight and thus out of consideration. They know I am quite safe to leave alone as I am no longer needed by them *or* by my people.

"My one problem is Mr. Lanier. I will remain greatly involved until such time as justice is served with that one!"

Nick nodded. He had to get to the station with Lanier's prints to figure his next step. He also had to set a little trap – with Det. Lt. Nick Storie as bait!

Chapter sixteen

"The prints were unquestionably Lanier's," Dr. Klein reported to Nick. "You knew they'd be. If that's all, I'm going to grab some rest. It's getting late."

"Thanks, Doc. I just have to work out a few little details, then I'm getting some rest myself. Ed Goins is handling homicide until my honeymoon's over.

"Some honeymoon, hunh?"

"You had to accept that place and obligate yourself. One day you'll learn!"

"There's no obligation, other than to solve the thing, which we've done. I want to tag Lanier before Pancho says my time limit's up."

"And before he blows some hick local-yokel cop's damned brains out for him?"

"That, too! Heard the tape, did you?"

"What tape to which dost thou refer? You know perfectly well nobody here has time to listen to all the evidence in somebody else's cases!"

He waved and went out.

Nick straightened the files and thought awhile, then went out himself. There was a cop on the roof to watch everything around since the bomb incident, so that wasn't a problem. He'd have to be careful at home.

Tomorrow was the day he hoped to get something to work from. Anything would do right now!

Judge Collins called Marsha at nine forty seven to say Jessup would be delivered to her courtroom promptly at ten fifteen. Marsha called Nick, who cleaned up and went to sit in the courtroom. The DEA wanted bail set, but Collins declared the fact she'd had to use virtual blackmail to get him there in the first place should show them there would be no bail set.

"You have the word of this department Agent Jessup will appear in court when summoned," Vernon, the DEA special attorney, argued. "The word of the federal government should be sufficient."

"I have sworn testimony from that same department of that same federal government already!" Collins snapped. "The net result of my accepting that word is why Agent Jessup is here before this court. We have direct evidence that testimony was sworn at a time there were already plans in place to contravene the terms of that testimony.

"In case you missed that day in first semester general law one oh one, that is perjury by definition!"

"Agent Jessup is only an agent of an operation of the federal government! He cannot give you the word of the government."

"But you, a lawyer for an agent of an operation of the federal government, *can*? How droll!

"Bail is denied! The charges are capital!"

"CAPITAL!?" Jessup cried.

"I suggest you allow any and all statements to be made by your legal counsel. According to evidence already presented for warrant there is a legally acceptable tape recording in which you state that the person you fraudulently caused to be released into your custody would commit a murder. That recording was made hours before petition for release. That makes you accessory to murder in the first degree, and murder in the first degree is generally considered a capital crime.

"You fled and went into hiding because your plans went awry. You had aid and abetment of the government agency your counsel now suggests I should trust to deal honestly with me. There is no reason to believe you will not again employ such crooked methods should an opportunity present itself. There is less reason to believe you would not be aided and abetted by that self-same government agency in fleeing prosecution.

"Bail is denied. Trial is set for April twenty second in this court.

"Bailiffs, remove Mr. Jessup to processing.

"Next case!"

Nick waited until the processing and booking were complete, then had Jessup brought to a visitors' room. Vernon came with him.

"So you're out to get the fed cop?" Jessup snarled.

"At least I didn't send some hick idiot cop to a drug lord's house to see if he'd get his stupid goddamned head blown off. We local-yokels down here never did do what you tried to manipulate us into, did we?"

"I have to respect your nerve if not you intelligence. I wouldn't have walked into DeGulio's place, announced I was a cop, and said I wanted to talk to him.

"He did that Vern. DeGulio thought it was so gutsy he bought this crud on the spot!

"So I also know who made the tape and when."

"You can think a little about something else. I'm still a cop doing his job while you're up for murder one and six or eight other things.

"Nobody bought me. Nobody can. Pancho and I get along. We like and respect each other. He does favors for me so long as they don't compromise his work or his honor. I do favors for him only so long as they don't compromise my job or honor.

"Mr. Vernon can explain honor to you if he has the time.

"I want Lanier. He put a bomb in my car. He killed Miss Sylvia Perez. Your using someone as stupid as Lanier makes me wonder about how the DEA selects its department heads."

"So? You want Lanier. Why tell me?" Jessup sneered.

"You have a way and place to contact him."

"Get your drug lord pal to find him."

"Mr. Vernon, there's something else about the tape you should understand if you're going to represent Agent Jessup," Nick stated, ignoring Jessup for the moment. "I know you'll get a copy, but you should know this now.

"Jessup several times made remarks about me being killed. Now the person he had released has killed one woman and has since attempted to kill me. I am going straight to Judge Collins from here if I don't get the information I want from Jessup. I will suggest the DEA might be making illegal deals with professional killers to hit local cops who get in their way.

"You may advise your client of his options. Bear in mind the kind of publicity this could generate."

"If I give you the information, what's my deal?" Jessup asked.

"Then I won't have to go to Judge Collins with the aforementioned suggestion. It saves the DEA a lot of bad publicity."

"No deal. I can ruin you! You got a little too cosy with a known drug dealer! A drug *lord*! The head of a whole drug syndicate with ties to three of the country's largest mafia-style families!"

"And I'll give the media a few facts about you and Pancho. Such as the fact your six years of investigation the taxpayers footed the bill for failed to give even the suggestion DeGulio is or ever was a drug supplier, dealer, or anything else vaguely illegal. His ties to any crime syndicates are merely speculations based on his associations with Alanza – who's known to be very hostile toward DeGulio.

"I'll go so far as to say that hostility never really

existed, either!

"Would it really surprise you to know DeGulio never was a drug lord, dealer, or head of anything, much less some national syndicate or cartel?"

"Crap! I watched him long enough to know exactly what he was doing."

"He was merely absorbing your attention, which kept it away from a certain few others. You never were too very smart. It was those others who were manipulating you. DeGulio found it convenient to allow himself to be used in that manner, because the one thing he *did* do was see that lots of money from those people went to his own people – very little to him.

"When you make your charges we'll tell the world about it. Pancho sees a lot of humor in the situation.

"I want Lanier!"

"Go to hell! I got nothing to say to you, hick! I'll chew you up and vomit you out!"

"Oh? You call Lanier stupid? He's out there and you're gonna face murder one charges.

"Think about it, you *bril*liant sophisticate! I have more than enough evidence to put you away for life without possibility of parole. I'm going to walk into that courtroom with that evidence I can present any way I see fit – and you sit there and try to bait me with insults? Me? The one who can ask DeGulio favors? Even that *he* testifies against you?

"Think of one other tiny little detail on my side. You'll be sitting duck duty right there among people you set up to get them *put* there.

"Yeah! *Bril*liant!

"Guards! Out!"

He walked out while Vernon tried to argue with Jessup. He knew Jessup had some way to contact

Lanier. The trap was loaded and set and Jessup was infuriated. Maybe he now would believe the case against him would weaken or fall apart if Nick wasn't around to testify.

Jessup had to know DeGulio's magnetic personality would make a complete fool out of him in any actual courtroom with a jury.

Would Jessup try to get Lanier to kill him?

Anything that might flush Lanier out would have to be tried. Nick didn't want him to decide to leave the area. This mess was ugly enough already.

Nick was at a disadvantage. He would have to force Jessup to act fast, before he thought. If he were to go to court the DEA could claim confidentiality for a lot of the testimony he needed. There was no doubt in his mind they'd try to get him off through any method they could find. They'd been given so much latitude by the courts already they tended to think they were above morality and the law.

A murder of innocent people because of a personal vendetta of one of their agents?

Those things happen.

The killing of a local cop because he could embarrass an agent and the department?

If that seemed "advisable."

There was a professional killer out there who was gunning for both Nathaniel Storie and Don Francisco DeGulio. Nick must never forget how serious that threat was or they'd both end up dead. The fact the killer wasn't entirely sane and wasn't very bright made the situation worse. He wasn't predictable for the very same reasons and was cunning. He didn't care who else got in the way or got hurt.

Was there another pressure point?

Nick grinned to himself and headed for Judge Collins' court. He might have one more little thing he could do!

"You want me to release Colton?" Judge Collins asked, looking at Nick shrewdly. "Why?"

"You've already figured that out. I have to get Jessup to panic and send Lanier after me. If Lanier leaves the state we'll never find him.

"If Colton suddenly gets released on a very low bail, Jessup starts worrying about what kind of side deal he's made. I made it pretty plain to Jessup that *he* wasn't getting any deals. We have him sewed up tight.

"You see, he let slip he knows we have a tape of his little conversation in Colton's office when I quoted some things that couldn't have come from anywhere else. If Colton's suddenly out on a low bond Jessup's going to start thinking maybe Colton saw how he was being set up to be the goat. Maybe Colton's as PO'ed about that as Jessup is at me, so what else does Colton know?

"Colton knows a hell of a lot too much! Jessup discussed this with him other times than at the office. He wouldn't have gotten Lanier out with no more than that.

"So! Colton's out and Jessup's head's suddenly in a vice!"

"I think the expression's something about his ass being in a crack. Now you're setting somebody up aren't you?"

"I intend to be there. As much as I could agree that Colton's being hit would save Florida taxpayers the expense of having to feed and house him for fifteen years, I don't believe in handling things that way.

"What if Lanier had the chance to get me, Colton, and DeGulio – at once?"

"Anybody else, I'd say you needed therapy. How do you work that part?"

Nick grinned and shook his head.

"Okay. I'll hold you fully responsible. Jessup, it was plain stupid, but I claim to have believed the US government wouldn't put someone like him in such a position. You I know. Your word's better than that whole crowd's sworn oath. I even think DeGulio's words better than any of theirs."

"Pancho's word's even better than mine. I'd stop short of dying to keep my word. He wouldn't."

"I'm only saying I'll try to keep anyone from being hurt. I'm not god. I can't guarantee even *I'll* survive this one!"

"Nick? Be careful," Judge Collins said seriously. "Good cops are hard to find anymore – besides, Marsha would never let me hear the end of it if you were to get murdered."

"I'll be as careful with this one as I ever was with anything in my life. I don't think I've ever been scared of anyone the same way I am of Lanier. Not like this. This isn't a healthy fear that keeps me alert. I'm afraid of him because I can't really predict what he might do. Other people who aren't involved could be hurt. Now I have to try to force him to do something I can predict exactly."

"You've predicted him very well so far," she said, studying Nick. "You do think he's insane, don't you?

"That could give him an out in court."

"He's to be tried in your court. You'd see he doesn't ever get back out. Yes. I think he's insane, but probably not in a legal sense. He's too cunning. He'll refuse that defense because it would make him face reality a little too directly."

She nodded. Again, she warned Nick to be careful.

That was one thing he fully intended!

Chapter seventeen

"Pancho, I want to set a bit of a trap," Nick said. "I want you to help me a little if you will."

Pancho was with Lonnie working at the Parks home. Nick would have thought him to be another of the hundreds of Latino workers in the area. Lonnie was working to one side of the lawn on a large bed of spathiphyllums and bromeliads. There were three area women standing by watching him work. He waved at Nick and answered a question from one of the women.

"They find very strange excuses to come wherever we're working at a given time. Lonnie likes the attention, I think, but he makes it plain there's nothing but talk if they're married.

"This morning a fellow they call Drums came by. He's almost as handsome as Lonnie. I thought there'd be a small riot! I find it incredible!

"So! What kind of trap?"

"Are the phone lines to your place in Boca Raton tapped?"

"I would think so. Routine," Pancho said, grinning. It looked strange through the large, bushy, false moustache.

"Then a call from you would get to Jessup fast?"

"Yes, but isn't he being detained?"

"Yeah, but you can bet someone's supposed to report to someone else whatever's said on that line."

"What do I do?"

"Call Ed or somebody and tell them you're planning on going back home tomorrow morning, but you have a meeting tonight at eight thirty with me and DEA Agent Colson. You don't know what it's about, but it's to be just the three of us. It's in a well-hidden place where you have my sworn guarantees about the information to be exchanged.

"All hints, no substance.

"Seeing as Colson's here, you wouldn't know much about him, right?"

Pancho nodded.

"You'll want a fast check so you'll know what to expect from Colson. You'll call back for the information at six."

"And?" Pancho asked, grinning, eyes sparkling with amusement.

"That's it. I handle it from there."

"So Lanier will hear from Jessup, who will hear it from their man in Miami. You will then go to a place where someone who looks like me and someone who looks like this Colson character will be waiting.

"Lanier wants me dead and he wants you dead, but who's this Colson?"

Nick explained what he'd done with Judge Collins and what he planned. Jessup would convince Lanier that Colson had to go along with Pancho and Nick, then the evidence against him wouldn't be strong enough to convict him of murder one.

Or something.

Jessup would very definitely have to get rid of Colson. That was a chance he dared not take. He knew full well Colson had the goods on him.

"I see," Pancho said when he'd finished. "Where do we go for me to call?"

Nick told Lonnie they'd be right back and took Pancho to the shopping mall a few miles away. He didn't want anyone to come too close when the number was traced.

As Pancho went to the payphone Nick said to throw in something about the police wanting him to meet him at their offices, but he had refused. He'd arrange a place and reveal where it was at the last minute so no one would be able to wire it.

Pancho gave Nick the high sign.

On the way back to the Parks job Pancho said Nick was to pick him up at five thirty so he could make the second call at six. Nick started to argue, but Pancho claimed the right to be there.

"We take Lanier alive and he goes on trial. That's something I need your word on, Pancho."

"Unless it somehow becomes a matter of another sort you have it, Nickie. That doesn't mean I won't defend myself, if it comes to that."

"Agreed! Five thirty at Lonnie's. You can make the call from the Circle K in Estero, then we'll go back to the station, then out to a place off Airport Road I have ready. We can see anything in any direction for more than a quarter mile."

"Fair enough. You know that amazing woman on the next block behind where we're working. She fixes coffee and cake. She says she won't play silly games about it, she likes to have Lonnie there because he gets her excited."

"Did Lonnie tell you about his finding a body in the vegetable bed in back? That's when I met him and Elise Norton (*Odd Jobs*)."

"She told me. She said her husband reaps the benefits of Lonnie getting her excited. Lonnie's her Pan. She hung that name on him."

Nick let Pancho out and headed for the station.

This had better work!

"Mad! This is totally insane!" Paddy cried. "You're not doing something for one of those idiotic TV shows!

"How do we work it?"

Marsha put in, "Maybe I could be there? I could be a recording secretary or something – and don't look at me like that! I know better!"

"We'll have to get Colson out of the way somehow," Jim Hill said. "If he's sitting in his apartment, Lanier'll know he ain't at no meeting on Airport Road. I'm close enough to his size that I can fool people at a distance, so we'll be able to pull it off IF we can convince Lanier it's him."

"I'll handle that!" Paddy promised. "I'll get Colson to come here and you can take it from there."

"How you gonna do that?" Marsha asked.

"What time?" Paddy asked Nick.

"He's got to be here at eight thirty."

Marsha handed Paddy the phone after a minute. Paddy said, "Mr. Colson? This is Capt. James James at police HQ. I need to talk with you about a few little items ... Mr. Colson, let me say it could prove greatly to your personal advantage to cooperate in this part ... Mr. Colson, it isn't *you* we're after!"

Paddy grinned at Nick and gave him the "V" sign, then, "Mr. Colson, you were merely a pawn. A setup. A goat. We're perfectly well aware of that ... If you wish to allow such an opportunity to pass...?"

He covered the mouthpiece and said, "He's hooked! He'll figure I want to make a deal." Then into the phone, "You can bring him if you like, of course. I suggest you consider who he works for – you? Or DEA?"

Another long pause.

"I will guarantee you there will be no recording of anything unless you request it. This will merely be a little discussion to determine whether or not there is a basis for presentation of information to Judge Collins. I'm sure she is fully aware of your situation. She is a very fair person, Mr. Colson. She wants what we want ... What?"

Marsha grinned and poured everyone more coffee.

"Mr. Colson, Judge Collins *is* furious! It's not directed at you personally, it's at Jessup ... Mr. Colson, we should not be discussing this matter over the telephone. Just remember that Judge Collins has your tape, so she *knows* who made the plan and she *knows* who manipulated her and the court.

"If you will ... How about eight o'clock tonight? Here?

"Perhaps you should be careful about your route and about who knows about it. Jessup's agent, Mr. Lanier is still at large ... No. Again, consider who *he* works for – and who he may report to ... Fine! Eight or a little before or after."

He hung up. "He'll be here around a quarter past eight or so. There's a sort of hollow ringing sound to his phone."

"That's because it's tapped," Marsha agreed. "I think those federal agencies spend half their time spying on each other and their own employees.

"Okay. We have to set this up tight. I have the regular police patrol around the mall watching to see who's watching the phones there around six. We have to get at least four men in place at that shop by five thirty. It wouldn't do for them to suddenly show up after there's any hint of where your trap's located.

"Remember how much Lanier likes bombs. Check your car if you stop anywhere. You can almost bet Lanier's going to be following you."

"Hey! Where did I lose control! Who made you department head?" Paddy demanded.

"Paddy, don't interrupt!" Jim replied reasonably. "This is important. Marsh always handles anything important!"

It was a joke among them that Marsha really ran the department – and many a truth is spoken in jest.

"I have to get Pancho to a phone at six, then I have to lose ... give me the phone.... No. They're at work," Nick said. "Damn! I'll be followed now!

"I have to get Pancho to a phone and I have to get him the directions to the meeting place."

"Nobody's going to be following me," Marsha said. "I'll leave at five like I always do. I can drive over to Lonnie's, carry Pancho to the phone at Estero, and give him a map.

"I can go home, fix Hank and the brats supper, and be back here by seven thirty.

"Nick, you're to stay among lots of people until we're ready to move on this.

"Now! Let's all sit around and pick holes in this so they can be patched up by party time!"

"It would seem that my *aide* has placed herself in full charge of operation "Dead End" – as we'll call it from now on," Paddy said happily. "All the screwups are to be directed to her file. All accolades, should this beat the odds and work, will be placed into *my* file!

"It's now four thirty two. I suggest all of you get some solid sustenance and get ready for a long night.

"Jim, maybe you should stay a bit out of sight yourself. You usually go home at six, so how do we work that?"

"Jenks is my size," Jim replied. "No one will be watching him, so he can put on my overcoat and drive off in my car.

"Nick, bring me back something from the restaurant. I'll call Eileen and tell her I'll be late."

They all went their own ways.

This hinged on one little item, and Nick had no way to

know if it was going to work. If Pancho's earlier call to Miami wasn't reported back to Jessup nothing was going to happen.

"A scummy-looking character's been hanging around close to the mall phones," Marsha reported. "Fred's thought he was a narc for a long time.

"You felt that was important, Nick?"

"If that phone's being watched they got the message from their tap in Boca Raton. Without that one single thing nothing else would happen. Now this might even work!

"Well, Pancho made his phone call. He's as charming as you said! I like him!

"Want to know where Lanier is right now?"

"You know?" Jim asked.

"They're not sure, but the guys say there's been a light in a window of a vacant office on the third floor of the Catherston Building. I don't think there'd be a chance of trapping him there. Way too much traffic. Way too dangerous.

"I *do* think you have to be very careful about a high-powered rifle up there when you go out.

"I've arranged for Frog to have the forensics van across from the door for when Colson gets here so he'll be shielded. It'll stay there until you and Jim leave. He'll see you, but the palms will stop him from having any clear shots at anyone except close to the door.

"He'll know about the guy on the roof from there, so that's why there weren't anymore bombs in cars."

"What if we can't match my clothes to whatever Colson wears when he comes in?" Jim asked. "It'll be bright enough to be sure he'd notice that."

"So you'll wear my grey overcoat," Paddy answered.

"It'll be obviously way too big, so we must be hiding what you're wearing."

Nick and Jim grinned.

"It's about time for Colson to get here," Marsha said. "Jim should stay out of sight from him, too."

They waited. About twenty minutes later Colson stopped across from the door and came in. Paddy invited him into his office. Marsha went to get them coffee and used a little device Crane had donated to the department. It could find any "bug" anywhere.

Marsha went back to the office with the coffee and said, "Mr. Colson, we'd appreciate it if you would honor the same terms we offered you. Please remove the bug and turn it off." She held up the BugChaser.

Colson grinned, pulled the broadcast unit from his inner coat pocket and handed it over to Paddy, who dropped it into a thick Styrofoam cooler after removing the batteries.

"Now! Anymore little devices?" Paddy asked. "Was the locator in the transmitter or separate?"

"There isn't any locator," Colson replied. "They can trace the bug."

Marsha grinned and moved the BugChaser around him. She stopped at his left pants pocket and raised an eyebrow. Colson looked surprised and fished everything out.

His car keys were on an old St. Christopher's medal. It was broadcasting a pulse every thirty seconds.

"Weak," Paddy said. "They have to within about six or eight hundred feet. They can activate it when they're close, so you're followed."

"Those slimy *bastards*!" Colson exploded. "I've carried that key chain for six years! Arnold Gaither gave it to me ... I'll be damned!

"I swear to you I never knew about that thing! I can't believe they've had me wired for the past six or seven years!

"Those slimy bastards!"

Paddy dropped the beacon into the cooler and carried it out to sit it on the wide rear bumper of the forensics van. He went back inside and sat across from Colson, looked over a sheaf of papers and said, "Mr. Colson, here's the deal.

"We have enough to hang you, but we know perfectly well it's a setup. That tape doesn't clear you. It does bring Jessup into it up to his crooked neck − which I fully intend to drop a noose around. It seems he's the slimiest bastard in a collection of slimy bastards.

"We have to go step-by-step through the time just after that tape was made until you got Lanier out of jail. That's the time Jessup arranged for the actual sequence of events that led to the murder of Sylvia Perez and the attempt on Lt. Storie's life here.

"It's quite obvious Jessup said and did things we know nothing about. Informing us of what those words and actions were will let you off the hook, I'm sure.

"Let me say right now we believe there is a plan by Jessup to kill you, Francisco DeGulio, and Lt. Storie. You protect Jessup at your personal peril. You were actually brought here for your own protection. It's part of a plan to force Lanier's hand, thus to get Jessup.

"I hate a crooked cop far more than a standard crook!"

Nick and Jim were just then getting into Nick's car.

Jim grinned and said, "Show time!"

Chapter eighteen

"What do you think Lanier's going to try?" Jim asked as they drove toward the old store where the trap was laid. "He's not too predictable, other than for his love of car bombs. He'll probably try one of those things he's seen on cheap TV shows. He's the type."

"Whatever it is, I hope the guys get him before he gets too close to us," Nick replied. "I've been in one shootout already, and that's more than enough. All it got me was a scar on my leg and a stay in the hospital"

"There's 'way too much firepower out there in the hands of that kind. All the training in the world's no good against some of those things."

Nick grunted. He was watching the rearview. "He's there. We've picked up a tail. Dark colored small truck. It's made the last two turns we made."

"Would Lanier know how to tail anyone?"

"He's probably got basic instructions.You can bet Jessop's bunch gave him a crash course. He's also got a neat little deal to follow the beacon I'm now carrying."

"Beacon?"

"Paddy put it in the cooler on the back of the lab van. Marsh used the BugChaser to find it. The van's the only place that's shielded from view. We didn't want him to give it to me inside because we didn't want Colson to see me around. That's why we came out so fast after Paddy went back in.

"It'll look like Colson went out there and waited a minute for me, then you came to the car with me and we left. I think we've timed it pretty good!

"Here's our turnoff. That'll be Pancho in Lonnie's work truck over there."

Nick flashed his headlights and Pancho fell right in behind them. They headed on for the vacant store and pulled into the lot in front. Jim and Nick got out and headed for Pancho, who was just getting out of Lonnie's truck. Nick glanced back along the road and suddenly yelled, "Down!"

He, Jim, and Pancho fell flat at about the same instant. There was a sudden rain of automatic weapons fire from the road behind them. A car suddenly blocked the exit road ahead by the loop from behind a Brazilian Pepper tree and another roared toward them from Airport Road.

"Down! Stay down!" Nick yelled. "Are you all right, Pancho?"

"Other than my hurt dignity I'm still fairly intact. All promises off, Nickie! The hijo de puta attacked me! We've all said he's stupid. I made it known absolutely years ago that attacking me is fatal!"

He slid back into Lonnie's truck.

Nick jumped for his car and Jim ran for the passenger door. Lanier was heading out across the field toward Airport Road. Nick radioed for the cars to block the entrance and exit roads because there was no other way out.

Lanier headed on toward Airport Road. He wasn't using his headlights, but they could see him from the surrounding glow from the overheads on Airport Road.

Pancho headed after him at an angle. There were fast flashes from Lanier's weapon, but he couldn't aim, so didn't come close to anyone.

Nick headed to the left to cut Lanier off. To the right was a bit too rough for the little light Toyota truck. Pancho suddenly floored Lonnie's old Dodge and came into the side and to the rear of the Toyota. Nick had to sluice around to avoid being hit head-on as the little truck spun halfway around and came directly at him.

Lanier continued the spin and headed toward Airport

Road again at an angle. Nick could see he had infra-red goggles on when they almost collided.

Pancho seemed to be giving Lanier some room toward the right, forcing the light truck onto the rougher ground. Nick stayed just behind so he couldn't cut back. Lanier didn't have the power to outrun either the Dodge or Nick's Pontiac.

Suddenly Pancho cut sharply toward Lanier, who twisted the wheel to the right – and ended up in the drainage canal beside Airport Road. The Toyota nosed downward and was sinking rapidly. Nick spun to a stop and jumped out just as Pancho did the same a few yards away. Jim kicked the door open and came up with his revolver aimed at the sinking truck. The two cars at the exits started toward them, one on the outside by Airport Road and one inside.

The door to the Toyota came open before the water reached half its height and Lanier dove out with an Uzi in one hand. The other hand was holding to the door frame.

Lanier swung the Uzi toward Nick and Jim as Pancho shouted a string of invective at him. He swung the weapon on around to fire at Pancho, who dropped. Jim fired one shot. Carefully.

Lanier screamed, dropped the Uzi, and thrashed around in the muddy ditch, clutching at his shoulder. He could barely reach the bottom of the ditch and keep his head out of the water.

"Come on out," Jim said. "Don't give me any excuse to put a few more holes in you. I'll enjoy doing it!"

"Don't kill him – yet," Pancho requested. "I want him to know intensity of pain. I want him to beg me to allow him to die!"

"I won't kill him," Jim replied. "I'll just shoot him a

few times in places that'll hurt."

Lanier worked toward the bank and climbed out, sobbing. Jim had hit him right in the shoulder joint.

He whined, "Don't kill me! Oh, god! I'm dying! Please don't kill me! I'll do anything you say! Don't kill me!

"I need a doctor bad! I'm bleeding to death! Oh, god!"

Pancho made a disgusted sound, then said, "Big macho man!

"If that's all you need me for here, Nickie? I'm actually becoming physically ill. He's so brave and bad so long as he's attacking old women!

"I don't want any revenge on him. He has to live with what he is. No one could find a harsher torture. He simply isn't worth the effort, is he? That's what you've tried to tell me since he killed Sylvie. He's simply not worth the contempt I feel.

"I'll allow your law to keep him alive a long time, knowing he will be strapped into your electric chair where a high voltage current will be passed through his jerking body until his soul's released to find the hell it will burn in for eternity!

"You could have gotten it easier until you put the bomb in Nickie's car, mierda! They'll fry your ass for trying to kill a police officer!

"You're right, Nickie. Anything I could do would be far too quick! There is no torture I could conceive of that would match having to live with knowing you are what he knows he is.

"I'll return Lonnie's shot-up truck to him. I'll buy him another if he'll allow it. This one has bullet holes all over it!

"So does your car, but that's what you get for using your personal vehicle in your work."

"It's not that easy," Nick grimaced. "Now we have to

go in to make statements and fill out forms."

"Nickie, I tried to tell you my way was better! Not so much complication! Just have the little punk go off somewhere and never come back! If your fellow officer shoots him in the crotch and we watch him flop around until he dies, do we still have to make statements and all that crap?"

"I'm afraid so. You'd have to fill out the forms explaining why we wasted the taxpayers' bullets."

"We could push him in the canal and hold him under," Jim said. "Don't say it! Then we'd have to fill out fifty dozen more forms for forensics! I know! They get you no matter *what* you do!"

Nick suddenly turned toward the sobbing Lanier. "How did DEA Agent Jessup get the word to you about our little meeting?"

"He called me from the payphone in the cellblock," Lanier said dejectedly. "He said you and Colson ... wait a minute! Where's Colson! This was a trap!"

"He's smarter than I ever thought!" Pancho said. "He figured out the obvious! It only took him half an hour!"

"I'll get you for this!" Lanier screamed. "This was a trap! You set me up! I'll get you for this!"

"Think about something!" Nick said quickly. "How about *Jessup* set you up? How else could *he* get off? He needed a goat, and you're *it*! If you managed to get the three of us they suddenly have nothing against *him*. We'd still have you for Sylvia Perez and that other attempt on me."

"Don't say anything else, Lanier!" Jim ordered. "Wait until you have a lawyer. Jessup wants you to run your mouth because it'll get *him* off!"

Lanier looked confused, then stared at Jim for a moment. He reached to touch his shattered shoulder, his eyes rolled up, and he passed out.

"Very good!" Pancho complimented. "You have ensured he will spill everything he knows about Agent Jessup.

"I'm Pancho. Nick hasn't introduced us. We can forgive the breach in manners, considering the unusual circumstances."

"Pancho, Jim. Jim, Pancho," Nick said. "Shall we call the lab to find the Uzi and pull that truck out of there? Then we can go fill out those forms.

"Carl, I'll allow you the pleasure of hauling that thing to the emergency room. Tell the doctors you're going to shackle him to the bed, then do it."

Sgt. Carl Hope nodded and said, "I called the lab and the EMS. That'll be one of them now."

They heard the sirens coming closer. Nick nodded and asked Pancho if he wanted to ride with him and Jim to the station. He said he was responsible for Lonnie's truck, so he'd follow them in.

Nick was dead tired. As soon as the EMS ambulance came and Carl and Lanier were aboard he went to his car. As he reached for the door handle he noticed blood on his sleeve.

"I'll be damned!" he cried. "I got shot and didn't even know it!"

Jim ran around to check. He insisted he'd drive Nick to the hospital.

"It's a scratch. You drive, but we can handle it with the kit at the office."

"Unh-uh!" Jim snapped back. "Hospital first. I'll tell Pancho where we're going."

"Damn it, Jim! Do you know how many extra forms we'll have to fill out if I go to the ... Right! If I'm hurt Marsh can fill out the forms and I'll just sign them!"

Jim told Pancho to go on to the station. He'd be there as soon as he took Nick to the emergency room for a quick patch-up job. Pancho was deeply concerned, but Nick convinced him it was only a scratch on his lower arm.

It was worse than that, but it wasn't too serious.

"They made me stay there overnight for this little scratch!" Nick complained next morning at the station. "What time did Pancho finally get away?"

"At six ten this morning," Jim replied. "I wish I'd've had the sense to get a scratch so I could get some sleep!

"Pancho's quite the character, isn't he?"

Nick grinned.

"Colson gave us some very good information," Paddy said. "He was royally pissed at the DEA for bugging him, and Jessup *was* trying to set him up.

"I think Lanier's going to spill a lot more than we'd hoped. He knows more than those people guessed.

"He's really nuts, you know. The way he sees it Jessup and his gangster friends set him up, so he's going to get his revenge in spades.

"Somehow he got the idea we were going to see he got the chair for trying to kill a cop. He's offering all kinds of deals.

"Collins is sending Beresford to handle it. She's going to wait until there won't be any question of shock reaction or drugs influencing his testimony, even though we've taken a lot of it already. We can compare what he's said already to what he says later and maybe determine which points he's stretching for his idea of revenge.

"He's completely incommunicado until the doctors declare him unaffected. Beresford's going to make a deal. Life or treatment in return for testimony against several people, Jessup being of primary concern.

"Beresford can tell him the insanity plea's simply to save his skin, so he'll go along. His knowledge about Doniletti and that Farris family means the feds will get him and give him relocation and protection. That shoulder's going to make it impossible to hide him, so he's not going to ever be a problem again, even if one of those gangs *doesn't* manage to get him.

"I think I agree with Pancho. He's so disgusting he was never worth our effort. If it wasn't that innocent people would be hurt I'd say to let him go and concentrate on the real scum, Jessup. The gangs would take care of Lanier fast enough."

"You sure are wound up!" Nick declared.

"Paddy can't refute most of Pancho's arguments," Marsha put in. "That worries him."

"The world's changed. We've gone a long way too far in a lot of directions, so it all begins to blur. Take a look at our leaders! Perjure yourself to congress and the court and you get pardons! The ones in position to pardon you *have* to do it to hide their own perjuries and even worse corruptions!

"Why is it the ones who always preach family values are the ones who do the most to destroy them? Are they so cynical about life they don't see they're the problem themselves? Don't they see what kinds of examples of everything mean and petty in the race they're examples of?

"When we look at Pancho DeGulio and see a man who's so truly concerned for people and who's sacrificed everything for them – legal or not – and compare him with someone like George Bush or Ronald Reagan who care only for power and money, what else can we believe but that somewhere it all went one eighty degrees from where we want to go?

"Tell the truth. Who's the hero to you among them?"

"*I'm* wound up?!" Paddy cried. "*Listen* to yourself!"

"I was listening to Nickie," Pancho said, stepping into the office. "I'm flattered in a way, but I don't think I appreciate much being included with any such sad comparison.

"George Bush, indeed! I have a *little* pride!"

Lonnie came in with Pancho. He said, "You should hear us argue at work! It's been great fun having Pancho around. He makes me think."

"I want to say one little thing myself," Janet said, stepping around the door. "You can argue and fuss all you like, but until we have a female president nothing's going to change.

"One more thing! This is supposed to be our honeymoon! You *will not* get involved in another shootout until such time as I say I'm tired of Nick! Is that *quite clear*?

"You! Nick! Home! Now!"

"We went to Sarasota and got her this morning," Lonnie said.

"I had to ride all the way back here in a truck full of bullet holes! I was mortified!" Janet said. "Now I see *my* car's full of bullet holes!

"Marsh, you haven't lived until you've ridden in that truck with Pancho on one side and Lonnie on the other!

"Nick? I either want you home, right now, or I'm filing for a divorce!"

"*I'm* wound up?!" Nick cried. "I have three hundred forms to fill out!"

"Just to sign. I filled them out," Marsha said. "I can see how that trip would make you more than ready for being alone with Nick!"

"Be like that Norton woman," Pancho said. "Let Lonnie excite you, then let Nick reap the benefits."

Nick looked around at these friends and felt a lump in his throat.

He was about as lucky as any man ever was.

Anywhere.

Anytime.

"Marsha, you and Hank have a good time at the place," Janet said. "I know you'll love it there. Lonnie'll be coming down in two weeks. Pancho's going with him. He can go now that he's no longer a part of that drug trade thing."

"And he can also go because his disguise is so good," Marsha replied. "Everybody thinks his name's Alizondro Vilas – which it is!

"What I don't understand is how his name can also be Pancho DeGulio! Legally!"

"Because my full name is Francisco Alizondro DeGulio Vilas," Pancho said. "It was generally written with my mother's maiden name represented with only the V. DeGulio was my father's sir name."

"So where does the Pancho come in?" Hank asked.

"Pancho's the nickname for Francisco," Nick replied. "You can also call him Cisco."

"Why not Frank?" Marsha asked.

"In Spanish-speaking countries the last part of a name is the nickname, not the first," Lonnie answered.

"So where does Pancho come in?" Hank asked again.

"The same place Betty comes from as a nickname for Elizabeth," Janet said. "They're calling your flight."

Marsha and Hank hugged everybody as Paddy came up with Jim. Paddy handed Marsha a basket with a big Bon Voyage ribbon on it. They all said goodbye again and Marsha and Hank went onto the plane. The rest went to the little airport restaurant where two waitresses almost got into a fight about who got to wait on them.

Lonnie was there.

Pancho shook his head and ordered breakfast for all of them. They chatted about various mundane things. The conversation inevitably got around to the trial the past week of Jessup.

"Colson was handled with a plea bargain and a deal and is now hidden somewhere by the feds," Paddy said. "I suppose we'll all be hearing a lot more from that one."

"You won't hear anything more," Pancho replied. "He's a major embarrassment to the department. He'll be put in a job somewhere where he can't do them anymore damage.

"Jessup looked awfully shocked when he was handed the life sentence first and the twenty years after. He expected concurrent sentencing so he could start appealing and stay out for a few years, then could have the rest dropped. Now he has no hope of getting out for thirty one years. He'll be seventy four, so that handles that!

"The one who interested me was Lanier."

"We'll all guarantee silence," Jim said. "Did you arrange that one?"

"No, my friends, I did not," Pancho replied sadly. "I wanted him to live in a complete hell until his trial, then to spend many years sitting in a cell despising himself for the whining little coward he really was.

"I think he got the infection from that ditch. It was stagnant water and there was raw sewage in it. It was probably a rather unpleasant sort of death. I do wish it could have been one where he was fully conscious through it all. The fear of death itself would have accomplished exactly what I wanted for that one!"

"He couldn't help what he was," Lonnie added. "I couldn't work up any sympathy for him, but I don't see anything right about a painful or lingering death. I think he was so pathetic that the quicker he died the better off the rest of the world was.

"We have to go, Panch. Alicia and Gloria are supposed

to meet us at ten. It's already eight thirty."

"I don't think I'll ever get used to this dating in the morning!" Pancho smiled. "It seems so strange! It's somehow not natural."

"Well, it's not really a date," Lonnie said. "We're just going to the beach, then to Jim's place on the island.

"We'll have your boat back by the time you get off duty, Jim.

"The dates are tonight, Panch. Shelly and Rosita."

Janet shook her head. "Lonnie, Pancho's not used to two women in one day. Especially not day after day!"

"Well, I can't work in three every day!" Lonnie returned with a wink at Nick. "I have to spend some time working. I promised those people I'd take care of their places."

"So you're dating again, Pancho," Paddy said. "That's good."

"It wasn't *my* idea!" Pancho cried. "Lonnie started giving me his leftovers, and I didn't know what else to do!"

"They all like Panch," Lonnie replied. "They get serious with him like they don't with me."

"Hah! They're serious as A-bombs with you!" Janet grinned. "They know better, so they take what they can get. Half a loaf and all that rot."

Nick looked around at them again. He squeezed Janet's shoulder and she smiled at him.

Yes. He was one lucky guy!

C. D. Moulton's works are available on most major outlets as printed or e-books. CD writes the CD Grimes, PI, mysteries, the Det. Lt. Nick Storie mysteries, the Clint Faraday mysteries, the Flight of the Maita science fiction series, books on orchid culture and many others of many types. Mystery, adventure, intrigue, science fiction, humor, fantasy, paranormal, mild erotica, and factual.

www.ingramcontent.com/pod-product-compliance
Lightning Source LLC
Chambersburg PA
CBHW052102150726
48002CB00002B/1001